Anonymous

Report of the Auditor of Accounts of the Commonwealth of Massachusetts for the Year Ending December 31, 1856

Anonymous

Report of the Auditor of Accounts of the Commonwealth of Massachusetts for the Year Ending December 31, 1856

Reprint of the original, first published in 1857.

1st Edition 2023 | ISBN: 978-3-37517-168-1

Salzwasser Verlag is an imprint of Outlook Verlagsgesellschaft mbH.

Verlag (Publisher): Outlook Verlag GmbH, Zeilweg 44, 60439 Frankfurt, Deutschland
Vertretungsberechtigt (Authorized to represent): E. Roepke, Zeilweg 44, 60439 Frankfurt, Deutschland
Druck (Print): Books on Demand GmbH, In de Tarpen 42, 22848 Norderstedt, Deutschland

REPORT

OF THE

AUDITOR OF ACCOUNTS

OF THE

Commonwealth of Massachusetts,

FOR THE YEAR ENDING

DECEMBER 31, 1856.

BOSTON:

WILLIAM WHITE, PRINTER TO THE STATE.

1857.

Commonwealth of Massachusetts.

AUDITOR'S OFFICE, BOSTON, }
January 13, 1857.

Hon. CHARLES A. PHELPS, *Speaker of the House of Representatives :—*

SIR :—I have the pleasure as well as duty, to transmit herewith, through you, to the Legislature, my Report as Auditor of the Commonwealth, for the year ending December 31, 1856,

And have the honor to be,

Very respectfully, your obedient servant,

C. R. RANSOM, *Auditor.*

Commonwealth of Massachusetts.

AUDITOR'S OFFICE, BOSTON,
January 13, 1857.

To the Honorable Senate and House of Representatives :—

In obedience to the requirements of law, I herewith present
to you my Report for the year 1856, it being the Eighth Annual
Report since the establishment of the office of State Auditor,
made in conformity with the fourth section of the fifty-sixth
chapter of the Act of 1849, which reads as follows :—

"The Auditor shall, annually, in the month of January,
carefully examine all the books and accounts of the Treasurer,
with all the vouchers of such accounts, and shall report thereon
to the legislature. He shall, on or before the fifteenth day of
January, annually, exhibit to the legislature a complete statement of the public property of the Commonwealth, its debts
and obligations of every kind, its revenue and expenses during
the preceding year, and the balance left in the treasury at the
close of such year, explaining whether such balance resulted
from an excess over current expenses, or otherwise. He shall
likewise submit, at the same time, an estimate of expenses for
the current year, distinguishing those which are ordinary and
current from those which are extraordinary, together with an
estimate of the ordinary income of the Commonwealth, and of
all other means which he may be able to point out for the
defraying of expenditures; and shall annex to the said state-
ments or estimates, such representations or suggestions as he
may deem necessary."

I shall avail myself of the privilege and duty imposed upon
me, by referring to some of the evils which appear to exist in

the various departments of the State Government, and which immediately affect the finances of the Commonwealth.

During the past year I have had occasion, in the official discharge of my duties, to make many revisions and call in question many accounts presented for allowance. This has not failed to cause much dissatisfaction on the part of those interested, some of whom, it is intimated, will apply to the legislature for additional remuneration. If such should be the case, I respectfully desire, as an act of courtesy and justice to myself, the privilege of presenting the reasons which have governed my action.

It is gratifying to state, that I have had the approval and co-operation of His Excellency the Governor, His Honor the Lt. Governor, and the Honorable Council, in the discharge of my official duties, at all times during the past year.

The Report will contain a statement of all the property of the Commonwealth, both productive and unproductive, with the amount of its debts and liabilities at the close of the year 1856,—the amount received into and paid from the treasury during the year, together with an estimate of the receipts and expenditures for the year 1857.

General Statement of Resources and Liabilities at the close of the year 1856, with the Receipts and Expenditures for that year, and an Estimate for 1857.

RESOURCES.

The property belonging to the Commonwealth on the 31st day of December, 1856, including the public buildings, funds, &c., amounts to the sum of $11,963,305.63.

Real estate, &c., unproductive, . . .	$2,853,997 24
Bonds and mortgages of railroads for scrip loaned, ...	5,049,555 56
Railroad Stock, Massachusetts School, and other funds, productive, ...	4,059,752 73
	$11,963,305 63

In addition to the above, the Commonwealth owns a large interest in the Back Bay lands, the value of which will depend very much upon the judicious action of the present legislature. The able Board of Commissioners, together with the Committee of the legislature of 1856, have devoted much time during the past year, in arranging plans, and in the settlement of past difficulties. They have succeeded, also, in fixing upon boundary lines to the entire satisfaction of all parties, so that the State is now in a fair way to realize an income from this source. The amount, however, will depend upon the wise and economical plan to be adopted for the management and disposition of the lands. By the Act of 1856, chap. 235, the first proceeds from the sale of these lands, is to be appropriated to the redemption of the three hundred thousand dollar six per cent. scrip, issued in 1856, and which becomes due July 1, 1862, '64, and '66.

LIABILITIES.

All the debts and liabilities of the Commonwealth amount to $7,597,680.56.

Scrip issued on account of the Reform School, State Prison, New Lunatic Hospital, State House, State Almshouses, and Loan of 1856,	$1,139,000 00
Scrip loaned sundry railroad corporations, payable by them, ...	5,049,555 56
Scrip issued to pay for 10,000 shares Western Railroad Stock, due in 1857, . . .	995,000 00
Temporary Loan, for money borrowed in anticipation of revenue and sale of scrip, . .	397,000 00
Amount due for interest on scrip, and not called for, 31st of December, 1856, . .	17,125 00
	$7,597,680 56

RECEIPTS AND EXPENDITURES.

The total receipts into the treasury for the year 1856, amounted to $2,495,676.51.

On account of ordinary revenue from Bank Tax, State Tax, Alien Passengers and Railroad Dividends, ...	$1,328,805 79

On account of Mass. School and other funds, principal and interest paid on notes, &c.,		$341,479 92
From sundry railroad corporations for interest on scrip loaned them,		52,500 00
Subscription to Reform School for Girls,		2,575 00
Five and six per cent. scrip sold,		370,000 00
Temporary loans, in anticipation of revenue and sale of scrip,		400,315 80
		$2,495,676 51

Cash on hand, 1st January, 1856—		
Borrowed in anticipation of revenue and sale of scrip,	$109,037 40	
Massachusetts School and other funds,	33,009 88	
Interest on railroad scrip,	15,075 00	
		$157,122 28
		$2,652,798 79

The total expenditures from the treasury for the year 1856, amounted to $2,507,955.54.

Pay of Council, Legislature, Salaries, State Paupers, State Printing, &c., &c.,		$1,335,096 45
Payments on account of Massachusetts School and other funds,		340,908 85
Interest on scrip loaned sundry railroad corporations,		52,675 00
Payments on account of Western Lunatic Hospital, Reform School for Girls, &c.,		113,622 44
Temporary loans repaid,		665,652 80
		$2,507,955 54

Cash on hand January 1, 1857—		
Borrowed in anticipation of revenue and sale of scrip,	$96,362 30	
Massachusetts School and other funds,	33,580 95	
Interest on railroad scrip,	14,900 00	
		$144,843 25
		$2,652,798 79

RECAPITULATION.

Total receipts, as above, ...	$2,495,676 51
Total payments, ...	2,507,955 54
Excess of payments, ...	**$12,279 03**

Receipts from ordinary revenue, . . .	$743,921 34
State Tax for 1855 and 1856, paid in, . .	584,884 45
	$1,328,805 79

Ordinary expenditure, . . $1,222,813 86		
Presidential Electors,	$233 60	
Census and Statistics,	32,350 34	
State House Enlargement, . . .	7,349 77	
State Prison, . .	9,200 00	
State Almshouses, .	32,000 62	
Taunton Hospital, .	9,846 13	
Industrial School, .	21,802 13	
	$112,782 59	
		$1,335,096 45
Excess of payments, ...		**$6,290 66**

GENERAL ESTIMATE FOR 1857.

The receipts on account of ordinary revenue for 1857, are estimated at		$767,716 05
The expenditures on account of ordinary revenue for 1857, are estimated at . . .		1,288,710 00
Showing a probable deficit of		$520,993 95
The unfunded debt amounted, January 1, 1857, to . .	$397,000 00	
The funded debt falling due Oct. 4, 1857, ...	25,000 00	
		422,000 00
		$942,993 95

To meet this there was cash in
　　the treasury, January, 1857,　　　$96,362 30
Western Lunatic Hospital Scrip,
　　upon which money is advanced,　　130,500 00
　　　　　　　　　　　　　　　　　　　　————————
　　　　　　　　　　　　　　　　　　　　　　226,862 30

　　　Amount to be provided for in 1857, .　.　$716,131 65

This is exclusive of the following railroad scrip, which becomes due within the present year, and will undoubtedly be taken care of by the several corporations at maturity:—

Eastern Railroad, due July 1, 1857,　　.　.　$100,000 00
Andover and Haverhill, due August 1, 1857, .　100,000 00
Norwich and Worcester, due July 15, 1857, .　400,000 00
And also of the Western Railroad Bonds, issued
　　to pay the Commonwealth's subscription for
　　stock, to meet which the Stock Sinking Fund
　　was established, due July 15, 1857,　.　.　995,000 00

RESOURCES, LIABILITIES, RECEIPTS AND EXPENDITURES, IN DETAIL.

RESOURCES.

The property of the Commonwealth, not including those funds which are appropriated for specific purposes, is as follows, viz. :—

State House and land,　　.　.　$500,000 00
Enlargement, to January 1, 1857,　243,103 86
　　　　　　　　　　　　　　　　————————
　　　　　　　　　　　　　　　　　　$743,103 86
Lunatic Hospital at Worcester,　　.　.　.　185,000 00
　　"　　　"　　　　Taunton, .　.　.　.　203,847 20
　　"　　　"　　　　Northampton, .　.　.　130,503 04
State Reform School for Boys, at Westboro', .　163,000 00
State Industrial School for Girls, at Lancaster,　41,927 13
State Prison at Charlestown, .　.　.　.　667,436 26

State Almshouse at Monson, .	$93,360 85	
"　　　" 　　Tewksbury,	90,990 71	
"　　　" 　　Bridgewater,	89,222 16	
"　　　" 　　Rainsford Island,	51,055 76	
		$324,629 48
State Arsenal at Cambridge, ...		281,754 18
House No. 12 Hancock Street, . . .		12,500 00
Warren Bridge, ...		50,000 00
Charles River Bridge, ...		25,000 00
Yacht Whisper, ...		2,650 00
Quit Claim Deed of Mr. Ambrose, ...		100 00
Weights, Measures and Balances, . . .		5,500 00
State Library, ...		17,046 09
		$2,853,997 24

The Commonwealth holds seven thousand and fifty-six shares of Western Railroad Stock, the par value of which is $705,600.

Also the rights in the Western Railroad Loan Sinking Fund belonging thereto, viz., $226,779.84.

These two last named sums, together with 2,944 shares Western Railroad Stock transferred to Massachusetts School Fund, by direction of the legislature of 1854, stand against a debt of $995,000, the payment of which is secured by the Western Railroad Stock Sinking Fund established by the Act of April 15, 1837, which fund now exceeds the necessary amount, as will be seen by the following statement:—

WESTERN RAILROAD STOCK SINKING FUND.

The amount standing to the credit of this fund, being for one-half the proceeds of the lands in Maine since April 15, 1837, is $1,110,064.37.

Notes for land in Maine sold, ...	$127,940 87
Scrip of State of Maine, 5 per cent., . .	125,000 00
Notes and Mortgages, ...	138,885 00
Notes with collateral and with sureties, . .	156,000 00
County, City, and Town Scrip, . . .	146,400 00
Western Railroad Stock, ...	94,300 00

Massachusetts 5 per cent. Scrip, . . .		159,202 28
Western Railroad Scrip, ...		118,000 00
Norwich and Worcester Railroad Scrip, . .		4,000 00
Andover and Haverhill Railroad Scrip, . .		2,000 00
Cash on hand on deposit, ...		8,028 20
		$1,079,756 35

To the above may be added the present value
of the rights in Western Railroad Loan Sinking Fund, belonging to 943 shares stock, . 30,308 32

    Total fund, January 1, 1857, . . . $1,110,064 37

Amount required to cancel scrip due July 15,
1857, ... 995,000 00

    Leaving a balance of $115,064 37

The Act of 1851, chapter 251, provides, that $100,000 of this sum shall be reserved for the redemption of scrip issued on account of the new Lunatic Hospital at Taunton. The balance can be used for any other purpose for which it may be required. The claim of the Commonwealth upon the General Government, for two-thirds of the sum, which was long since acknowledged to be due to this State and Maine, say about $181,000, also belongs to this Fund.

STATE ALMSHOUSE LOAN SINKING FUND.

By the Acts of 1852, chapter 275, and 1854, chapter 355, $6,000 is to be reserved, annually, from the amount received from Alien Passengers, to constitute a fund for the payment of the State Almshouse Loan.

This now consists of

Massachusetts 5 per cent. Scrip, . . .		$15,000 00
Note of the town of Brookline, . . .		6,000 00
Cash on hand, ...		1,609 29
		$22,609 29

Cash on hand January 1, 1857,
To pay interest on Railroad Scrip—
Andover and Haverhill, $1,300 00
Eastern,　　　.　　.　　3,100 00
Norwich and Worcester, 10,500 00
　　　　　　　　——————— $14,900 00
Borrowed in anticipation of revenue
　　and of the sale of scrip, .　　. 96,362 30
　　　　　　　　———————　　　$111,262 30

Total property, productive and unproductive,
　　except the funds, the income of which is
　　specifically appropriated, .　　.　　.　　. 5,211,313 04
Total debt of the Commonwealth, not includ-
　　ing liabilities on account of scrip loaned, . 2,548,125 00
　　　　　　　　　　　　　　　　　　————————
　　Balance,　　.　.　.　.　.　. $2,663,188 04

BONDS AND MORTGAGES OF RAILROAD CORPORATIONS.

The Commonwealth holds as security, for the final payment
of scrip loaned to sundry railroad corporations, a mortgage on
each of the roads, and shares of stock in all but the Western.

Western Railroad Sterling Bonds—
Mortgage, April 20, 1838,　　. $2,100,000 00
　　"　　　"　　10, 1839,　　. 1,200,000 00
　　"　　　July 13, 1841,　　. 　700,000 00
　　　　　　　　　　　　　　————————
　　　　　　　　　　　　　　$4,000,000 00
　　Less £100 not issued,　　.　　444 44
　　　　　　　　　　　　　　————————　$3,999,555 56

To the above should be added, for exchange
between Federal and Sterling currency, about
$320,000.
　　Andover and Haverhill Railroad—
Mortgage, May 1, 1837, .　　. $100,000 00
　　Boston and Portland Railroad—
Mortgage, September 27, 1839,　50,000 00
　　　　　　　　　　　　　　————————
　　　　　　　　　　　　　　　　150,000 00

Both the above are now Boston and Maine.

Eastern Railroad—
Mortgage, August 23, 1837, ... $500,000 00
   Norwich and Worcester Railroad—
Mortgage, May 1, 1837, ...   400,000 00
                                            $5,049,555 56

The shares of stock held as additional security are as follows, viz. :—

Andover and Haverhill, ...   1,000 shares.
Eastern, ...   3,000   "
Norwich and Worcester, ...   4,000   "

The above-named shares are liable to be sold upon failure to make prompt payment of principal or interest of the scrip as it falls due.   The interest has always been punctually paid by these corporations.

MASSACHUSETTS SCHOOL AND OTHER FUNDS, IN DETAIL.

The following is a detailed account of the various funds belonging to the Commonwealth, the income of which is specifically appropriated.

MASSACHUSETTS SCHOOL FUND.

This fund was established in 1834, when it was provided that one-half of all the moneys received for sales of lands in Maine, should be added to the amount received of the General Government in 1831, and the income thereof annually apportioned among the towns of the Commonwealth for the support of common schools.

It was provided by the Act of 1846, chap. 219, that all charges for educational purposes should be paid from the principal of this fund, which provision retarded its increase until 1853, when the sale of the remainder of the lands in Maine added to the fund about $323,000.

In conformity with the Act of 1854, chap. 300, the Treasurer of the Commonwealth transferred to this fund 2,944 shares Western Railroad Stock, and by the provisions of said Act, all charges for educational purposes are paid from one-half of the annual income of the fund, and the other half apportioned and distributed equally among the cities and towns, for the support of common schools, in the manner heretofore provided for the distribution of the whole income.

Notwithstanding the large amounts annually paid from the treasury on account of educational expenses, from one-half of the income of this fund, yet the principal is gradually increasing by the addition of the yearly surplus from the income.

The funds are now invested as follows:—

Notes for land in Maine,	$127,940 87
State of Maine 5 per cent. Scrip,	125,000 00
Massachusetts Scrip,	80,797 72
Railroad Scrip,	260,000 00
Notes and Mortgages,	144,050 23
County, City, and Town Scrip,	292,570 00
Notes with collateral and with sureties,	109,000 00
Western Railroad Stock,	376,500 00
Cash on hand,	1,053 00
	$1,516,911 82

To this may be added the rights in Western Railroad Loan Sinking Fund, belonging to 3,765 shares stock, present value, $121,109 50

$1,638,021 32

INTEREST ON SCHOOL FUND FOR 1856.

Cash in the hands of Treasurer, $20,349 83

This sum, together with the amount to be received up to June 1, 1857, will be equally divided according to the provisions of the Act of 1854, and one-half will be apportioned and paid to the several cities and towns of the Commonwealth on the 10th of July.

SCHOOL FUND FOR INDIANS.

Amount reserved from the surplus revenue, as per Act of 1837, chap. 85, for the benefit of schools among certain Indian tribes, invested in note of the town of Winthrop, $2,500.

TODD NORMAL SCHOOL FUND.

Amount invested in note of the county of Worcester, ...	$10,800 00
Note of town of Winthrop, ...	1,100 00
	$11,900 00

Interest on School Fund for Indians, cash on hand, ...	$75 00
Interest on Todd Normal School Fund, cash on hand, ...	145 00

HASSANAMESSETT INDIAN FUND.

Cash in Treasurer's hands, ...	$162 50

CHARLES RIVER AND WARREN BRIDGE FUND.

The balance now standing to the credit of this fund, is	$2,301 68

The cost of rebuilding the Charles River Bridge, and repairing the Warren Bridge, has now been paid from the receipts for tolls upon said bridges, except one claim for land-damages, amounting to $9.018.49 ; after this sum has been paid, the fund will begin to accumulate until it reaches the sum of one hundred thousand dollars, after which, by the Act of 1854, chap. 451, the bridges will be free.

These are all the funds in the hands of the Treasurer of the Commonwealth, excepting the Western Railroad Loan Sinking Fund, belonging to the Western Railroad Corporation, which will be noticed hereafter.

STATE REFORM SCHOOL FUND.

Amount placed in the hands of the Treasurer
of the institution, ... $20,000 00

MARSHPEE INDIAN FUND.

Amount placed in the hands of the Treasurer
of the tribe, ... $6,000 00

NATICK INDIAN FUND.

Amount placed in the hands of their Guardian, $1,125 15

RECAPITULATION.

Massachusetts School Fund, ...	$1,638,021 32
Interest on School Fund, ...	20,349 83
School Fund for Indians, ...	2,500 00
Todd Normal School Fund, ...	11,900 00
Interest on School Fund for Indians, . .	75 00
Interest on Todd Normal School Fund, . .	1 45
Hassanamessett Indian Fund, . . .	162 50
Charles River and Warren Bridge Fund, .	2,301 68

Funds in the treasury, ... $1,675,311 78

Reform School Fund, . .	$20,000 00	
Indian Funds, . . .	7,125 15	
		27,125 15

$1,702,436 93

Railroad bonds and mortgages brought forward,	5,049,555 56
Productive property of the Commonwealth, .	2,357,315 80
Real estate, &c., unproductive, . . .	2,853,997 24

$11,963,305 53

Debts and liabilities, ... 7,597,680 56

Surplus, ... $4,365,624 97

DEBTS AND LIABILITIES OF THE COMMONWEALTH, IN DETAIL, AT THE CLOSE OF THE YEAR 1856.

The total liabilities of the Commonwealth, as has been stated generally, amount.to $7,597,680.56

1. Scrip loaned to sundry railroad corporations, payment of which is secured by mortgage of their several roads.

Western Railroad Sterling Bonds—

Due April 1, 1868, . .	£135,000 00	
" Oct. 1, 1868, . .	337,500 00	
" Oct. 1, 1869, . .	90,000 00	
" April 1, 1870, . .	180,000 00	
" April 1, 1871, . .	157,400 00	
	£899,900 00	$3,999,555 56

Eastern Railroad, (dollar bonds)—

Due July 1, 1857,. . . .	$100,000 00	
" Sept. 1, 1858,. . . .	100,000 00	
" April 1, 1859,. . .	300,000 00	
		$500,000 00

Norwich and Worcester Railroad—
Due July 15, 1857, ... $400,000 00

Andover and Haverhill, (now Bos. and Maine)—
Due August 1, 1857, ... $100,000 00

Boston and Portland, (now Boston and Maine)—
Due August 1, 1859, ... $50,000 00

Total scrip loaned, ... $5,049,555 56

Interest at five per cent. on the Western, is payable by the corporation in London, or at their office in Boston ; on all the others interest is paid by the Treasurer of the Commonwealth.

2. Western Railroad, dollar bonds, issued to pay the Commonwealth's subscription for ten thousand shares stock, due July 15, 1857, ... $995,000 00

3. State Scrip, issued to pay for public buildings, and for temporary loans:—

State Reform School, 5 per cent. Scrip—
Due Oct. 4, 1857,.　　.　　,　　$25,000 00
  " July 1, 1860,.　　.　　.　　 75,000 00
　　　　　　　　　　　　　　　　　　　　　$100,000 00

State Prison Scrip, 5 per cent.—
Due Dec. 1, 1860, .　.　.　:　.　.　$100,000 00

Lunatic Hospital (Taunton) 5 per cent. Scrip—
Due April 1, 1865,　　.　.　　$70,000 00
  " Nov. 1, 1865,　　.　.　　 100,000 00
　　　　　　　　　　　　　　　　　　　　　$170,000 00

State Almshouse Scrip, 5 per cent.—
Due Nov. 1, 1872, .　.　.　$100,000 00
  " Oct. 1, 1873, .　.　.　 60,000 00
  " Oct. 1, 1874, .　.　.　 50,000 00
　　　　　　　　　　　　　　　　　　　　　$210,000 00

Enlargement of the State House 5 per cent Scrip—
Due Oct. 1, 1873, .　.　.　$65,000 00
  " Oct. 1, 1874, .　.　.　 100,000 00
　　　　　　　　　　　　　　　　　　　　　$165,000 00

Lunatic Hospital (Taunton) and State Prison 5 per ct. Scrip—
Due July 1, 1874, .　.　.　.　.　.　$94,000 00

6 per cent. Scrip of 1856—
Due July 1, 1862, .　.　.　$100,000 00
  " July 1, 1864, .　.　.　 100,000 00
  " July 1, 1866, .　.　.　 100,000 00
　　　　　　　　　　　　　　　　　　　　　$300,000 00
　　　　　　　　　　　　　　　　　　　　$1,139,000 00

Temporary loans for money in anticipation of revenue and the sale of scrip, .　.　.　.　.　.　$397,000 00

Sums due from the treasury, and not called for on the 31st of December:—
Interest on Western Railroad
  Scrip, .　.　.　.　.　$525 00

Interest on Almshouse Scrip, 1852,	$250 00	
Interest on Lunatic Hospital and State Prison Scrip, . .	225 00	
Interest on State House Enlargement Scrip, ...	325 00	
Interest on 6 per cent. Scrip of 1856, ...	900 00	
Interest on Andover and Haverhill Railroad Scrip, . .	1,300 00	
Interest on Norwich and Worcester Railroad Scrip, . .	10,500 00	
Int. on Eastern Railroad Scrip,	3,100 00	
		$17,125 00
Total debts and liabilities, . . .		$7,597,680 56

During the year, the funded debt of the Commonwealth has been increased $370,000, by the issue of scrip for the " Lunatic Hospital and State Prison," " State House Enlargement," and " 6 per cent. of 1856 " Loans, while the Temporary Loan has been reduced $265,337.

The amount of scrip still unsold, is $150,000, authorized for the building of the Western (Northampton) Lunatic Hospital.

RECEIPTS AND EXPENDITURES FOR 1856, IN DETAIL.

RECEIPTS.

Bank Tax.　Rev. Stat., ch. 9.

Received from Boston Banks, .	$321,100 00	
" " country " .	262,345 43	
		$583,445 43

State Tax.　Act 1856, ch. 223, and 1855, ch. 461.

Received on account of tax due Dec. 1, 1855, . . .	$55,974 50	
Received on account of tax due Dec. 1, 1856, . . .	528,909 95	
		584,884 45

Alien Passengers. Act. 1848, ch. 313.

Received from A. G. Goodwin,
Superintendent at Boston, . $16,810 68
Received from J. G. Edwards,
Superintendent at N. Bedford, 68 00
$16,878 68

Attorney for Suffolk County. Act 1839, ch.
136.

Received from George W. Cooley,
for forfeited recognizances, ... 529 97

Insurance Tax. Act 1852, ch. 231, and Act
1854, ch. 453.

Received from Agents of foreign Insurance
Companies, ... 3,312 13

Hawkers and Peddlers. Act 1846, ch. 244.

Received from the Secretary of
State, fees received by him for
1855, ... $308 00
Received from the Secretary of
State, fees received by him to
December 31, 1856, . . 213 00
521 00

Alien Estates. Rev. Stat., ch. 61.

Received from F. E. Parker, . $533 69
"   "   W. Jennison, . 358 63
"   "   Thomas Nedham, 74 45
966 77

Stationery.

Received from H. A. Marsh, clerk of the House
of Representatives for 1855, for overpayment
on account of stationery, ... 996 00

Courts of Insolvency. Act 1856, ch. 284.

Received for fees of all the Courts to October
1, 1856, ... 195 00

Charles River and Warren Bridge. Act 1854, ch. 451.

Received for amount advanced from ordinary revenue in 1854–5, ...	$9,530 25

Per cent. on State Tax.

Received from sundry towns for delinquency,	798 13

State Printing.

Received from School Fund for printing in 1855,	2,533 44

Income of Western Railroad Stock Sinking Fund. Act. 1850, ch. 189.

Received for interest and dividends belonging to this fund, ...	52,870 99

Western Railroad Dividends. Act 1837, ch. 172.

Received January, 1856, . .	$24,696 00	
" July, 1856, . .	24,696 00	
		49,392 00

Interest on Deposits.

Received on account of money deposited in bank,	1,620 69

Accrued interest on Scrip sold.

On 6 per cent. Scrip of 1856, .	$4,349 15	
On State House Scrip of 1854, .	6,743 89	
On Lunatic Hospital and State Prison Scrip of 1854, . .	85 13	
		11,178 17

Premium on Scrip sold.

On 6 per cent. Scrip 1856, ...	7,633 50

Salaries.

Secretary's fees, ...	1,247 62

Sundry accounts.

Sundry over allowances refunded, . . .	271 57
Total Ordinary Revenue, . . .	$1,328,805 79

Temporary Loans. Resolves 1856, ch. 3 and 64.

Amount borrowed as above, ...	400,315 80

State Loans.

Lunatic Hospital and State Prison 5 per cent. Act 1854, ch. 430,	$1,000 00	
State House 5 per cent. Act 1854, ch. 454,	69,000 00	
Six per cent. Scrip, 1856. Act 1856, ch. 235,	300,000 00	
		$370,000 00

Western Railroad Loan Sinking Fund. Act 1838, ch. 9.

Annual contribution from Western Railroad, 1 per cent. on loan,		40,000 00

Western Railroad Stock Sinking Fund. Act 1837, ch. 172.

One-half received for land notes paid in,	$3,580 92	
One-half received for sale of lands,	125 00	
Principal on loans paid in,	81,419 00	
		85,124 92

Massachusetts School Fund. Rev. Stat., § 13.

One-half amount received for land notes paid in,	$3,580 92	
One-half amount received for sales of lands,	125 00	
Balance of income paid in,	1,534 97	
Principal on loans paid in,	21,886 27	
		27,127 16

Interest on School Fund. Acts 1849, ch. 117 ; 1854, ch. 300.

Received to June 1, 1856,	$36,874 56	
"　　since June 1, 1856,	47,752 93	
		84,627 49

Interest on School Fund for Indians. Act 1837, ch. 85.

Interest on this fund,		225 00

Interest on Todd Normal School Fund. Act 1850, ch. 88.

Received for interest on investments,		715 45

State Almshouse Loan Sinking Fund.　Acts
1852, ch. 275, and 1854, ch. 355.

Received from Alien Passenger account,	$6,000 00	
Received from principal of loan paid in,	3,075 00	
Received interest on investments,	845 04	
		$9,920 04

State Reform School for Girls.　Act. 1855,
ch. 442, and Resolve 1855, ch. 83.

Received for subscription,	2,575 00

Charles River and Warren Bridge Fund.
Act 1854, ch. 451.

Received of Jeremiah S. Remick, to Dec. 1, 1856,	90,123 62

Interest on Scrip loaned.

Andover and Haverhill Railroad,	$5,000 00	
Boston and Portland Railroad,	2,500 00	
Eastern Railroad,	25,000 00	
Norwich and Worcester Railroad,	20,000 00	
		52,500 00

School Fund for Indians.

Received on account of loan paid in,	2,500 00

Hassanamessett Indian Fund.

Received two years' interest on the above fund,	16 24

Todd Normal School Fund.

Amount of loan paid in,	1,100 00
	$1,166,870 72

Receipts on account of Ordinary Revenue, as before stated,	$1,328,805 79
	$2,495,676 51

Cash on hand January 1, 1856, on account
of School and other funds,

School Fund, ...	$1,925 84	
Western Railroad Stock Sinking Fund, ...	303 28	
Hassanamessett Indian Fund, .	162 50	
Income Mass. School Fund, .	29,929 01	
State Almshouse Loan Sinking Fund, ...	689 25	

On account of Scrip.

Andover and Haverhill Railroad,	1,125 00	
Eastern Railroad, . . .	3,250 00	
Norwich and Worcester Railroad,	10,700 00	
Cash on hand, borrowed in anticipation of revenue and sale of scrip, ...	109,037 40	
		157,122 28
		$2,652,798 79

PAYMENTS.

Legislative and Executive.

Council. Resolve 1856, ch. 83.

Pay for services, ...	$8,448 00	
Pay for travel, ...	1,891 00	
		$10,339 00

Senate.

Pay of 40 members for services, ...	$19,296 00	
Pay of 40 members for travel, ...	387 00	
		$19,683 00

House of Representatives.

Pay of 329 members for services, . . .	$153,714 00	
Pay of 329 members for travel, ...	3,077 00	
		156,791 00

Pay of Clerks and Assistants of Senate and House of Representatives, .	7,050 00	

Pay of Chaplains, Senate and House of Representatives, .	$400 00	
Pay of Doorkeepers, Messengers and Pages, ...	8,930 00	
Pay of Witnesses before Committees, ...	275 86	
Travelling expenses of Committees, ...	3,017 96	
Sickness and funeral expenses of members, ...	654 20	
Filing Documents, . . .	897 75	
Books, ...	1,151 18	
Postage, ...	304 58 ·	
		$199,155 53

Salaries.

Pay of the Executive, Judiciary, &c., from Oct. 1, 1855, to Oct. 1, 1856, . . .	114,854 94

Fuel and Lights. Resolve 1855, ch. 57.

Paid for Wood, Coal, Gas, &c., . . .	2,647 97

Furniture. Resolves 1853, ch. 81–87, and 1856, ch. 32.

Paid for Furniture for the various Departments,	8,113 94

Repairs. Resolve 1856, ch. 98.

Paid for Repairs upon and about the State House, ...	16,615 69

Stationery. Resolves 1846, ch. 75, 1856, chaps. 74 and 95.

For the Legislature and the various Departments, ...	8,744 73

State Library. Rev. Stat., ch. 11, sec. 12, and Resolves 1854, ch. 76, 1852, ch. 16, 1856, ch. 27.

	3,692 76

Newspapers and Advertising. Resolves 1846, ch. 75, 1855, ch. 53, 1856, chaps. 74 and 93, and Order of both branches.

Newspapers for members of the Legislature, advertising, &c., ...	8,854 61

State Printing. Resolves 1852, ch. 9, 1855,
      ch. 49, and 1856, ch. 74.
Paid Wm. White for printing for Legislature
   and the various Departments, .   .   ·. $47,616 28

Postage. Resolve 1810, ch. 95.
Paid from Oct. 1, 1855, to Oct. 1, 1856, .   .   1,583 87

Sheriffs. Rev. Stat., ch. 12, sec. 5.
Paid for returning votes, &c., ...   736 60

Indexes and Journals.
Paid P. L. Cox, for duplicate
   Senate Journal for 1855, per
   Resolve 1855, ch. 55, . - . $300 00
Paid P. L. Cox, for duplicate
   Senate Journal for 1856, per
   Resolve 1856, ch. 83, . .   300 00
Paid P. L. Cox, as per Resolve
   1856, ch. 102, for Catalogue
   and Index of the Senate files,   760 00
Paid W. E. P. Haskell, Resolve
   1856, ch. 40, for preparing the
   General Index of the Journals
   of the House, and preparing a
   Catalogue of the papers on file,
   &c., ...   2,803 00
Paid N. B. Shurtleff, Order Governor and Council, Resolve
   1855, ch. 19, for his services in
   supervising the publication of
   the Colony of New Plymouth
   Records, ...   2,500 00
Paid for services copying Records
   of the Colony of New Plymouth,
   as per Resolves 1854, ch. 5,
   and 1855, ch. 19, .   .   .   4,019 00
Paid Wm. White, Resolve 1855,
 . ch. 19, for Stereotyping 6 vols.
   General Court Records, .   .   7,112 10

Paid E. Pulsifer, Resolve 1856, ch. 49, services on Gen. Court Records, ...	$60 00	
Paid W. S. Russell, Resolves 1852–5, ch. 86, 75, indexing Old Colony Records, . .	1,200 00	
Paid W. E. P. Haskell, Order of House 5th of June, 1856, .	142 00	
		$19,196 10
Contingent Fund.　Resolve 1856, ch. 103.		
Paid to the Sergeant-at-Arms, . . .		2,500 00
Bank Commissioners.　Act 1851, ch. 127.		
Paid three Commissioners for services, ...	$5,960 00	
Paid three Commissioners for travel, ...	1,023 85	
		6,983 85
Insurance Commissioners.　Act 1855, ch. 124, Resolves 1855, ch. 77, and 1856, ch. 95.		
Paid three Commissioners for services, ...	$4,600 00	
Paid three Commissioners for travel, ...	845 50	
Paid for office expenses, stationery, &c., ...	1,838 90	
		7,284 40
Commissioners for various purposes, . .		4,446 89
Legal counsel paid, ...		300 00
Indemnification to Officers.　Act 1855, ch. 271.		
Paid sundry persons, ...		8,322 84
Presidential Electors.　Rev. Stat., ch. 6, sect. 23.		
Paid for attendance and travel, . . .		233 60
Annuity to Harvard College.　Resolve 1847, ch. 98.		
Paid in full under this Resolve, . . .		666 66

Land Office.   Act 1851, ch. 190.
Paid the Agent his salary to Oct. 1, 1856,   . $1,000 00

Weights, Measures and Balances.   Act 1850, ch. 195.
Paid for new town, ...   157 00

Courts of Insolvency.   Act 1856, ch. 284.
Paid fourteen Judges their sala-
    ries to Oct. 1, 1856,   .   . $4,045 44
Paid fourteen Registers their
    salaries to Oct. 1, 1856, .   .   2,748 82
Paid expenses of the Courts to
    Oct. 1, 1856, ...   330 17
                                        ————
                                                    7,124 43

Census and Statistics.   Act 1856, ch. 48.
Paid to cities and towns throughout the Com-
    monwealth, for Agents employed on said work,   32,350 34

Term Reports,
Paid as above, ...   2,214 10

Charitable.

Asylum for the Blind.   Resolve 1855, ch. 62.
Paid to the Treasurer of said institution,   . $12,000 00

School for Idiots.   Resolve 1851, ch. 44.
Amount paid to said institution,   .   .   .   5,000 00

Asylum for Deaf and Dumb.   Resolve 1829,
    ch. 41, 1837, ch. 79, and 1847, ch. 94.
Paid for board, clothing and tuition to April 1,
    1857, ...   8,909 33

Eye and Ear Infirmary.   Resolve 1853, ch. 40.
Paid to said institution, ...   2,500 00

Expenses Taunton Lunatic Hospital.   Act
    1853, ch. 318, and Resolve 1855, ch. 42.
Paid salary of Officers to Oct. 1,
    1856, ... $2,920 98

Paid for books for library for use
of inmates, ... $150 00

                                       $3,070 98

Expenses Worcester Lunatic Hospital. Rev.
Stat., ch. 48.

Paid salary of Officers to Oct. 1, 1856, .   .   2,775 00

Annuity of Martha Johonnot.   Resolve 1841,
ch. 65.

Paid to sundry persons, ...   1,640 00

Coroners.   Rev. Stat., ch. 140.

Paid sundry coroners for expense of holding
inquests, ...   1,959 36

Pensioners.

Paid under sundry Resolves, ...   1,370 20

Alien Commissioners.   Act 1851, ch. 342.

Paid three Commissioners for services, ... $1,343 33

Paid office expenses, .   .   .   1,786 06

Paid agents services and expenses
visiting cities and towns, &c.,   3,180 69

Paid agents for the various railroad stations,   .   .   .   4,927 00

                                       11,237 08

Expenses State Almshouses.   Act 1854, ch.
189 and 262 ; Resolve 1855, ch. 42.

Paid Superintendent at Tewks-
bury, 12 months to Dec. 1, 1856, $51,919 14

Paid Superintendent at Bridgewa-
ter, 12 months to Dec. 1, 1856,   33,091 72

Paid Superintendent at Monson,
12 months to Dec. 1, 1856, .   53,515 97

Paid Superintendent at Rainsford
Island, 12 months to Oct. 1, 1856,   32,838 75

Paid twelve inspectors for their
services, ...   1,554 22

Paid twelve inspectors for travel-
ing expenses,   .   .   .   645 33

                                     173,565 13

Indians. Act 1850, ch. 141, and Resolve 1855, ch. 20.

Paid, ... : $2,654 60

Alien Passengers. Acts 1852, ch. 275, and 1854, ch. 355.

Paid to State Almshouse Sinking Fund, . . 6,000 00

State Paupers.

Paid to the several cities and towns for support and burials, ... 66,878 06

Scientific and Educational.

State Maps and Surveys. Resolve 1852, ch. 28.

Paid, ... $18 20

Agricultural Societies. Rev. Stat., ch. 42, . Acts 1855, ch. 278, Acts 1856, ch. 25 and 126.

Paid bounty to twenty-two societies, . . 11,684 76

American Institute of Instruction. Resolve 1851, ch. 35.

Paid annual appropriation, ... 300 00

State Board of Agriculture. Act 1852, ch. 42, Resolve 1853, ch. 67. Resolves 1854, ch. 72 and 33, 1856, ch. 65.

Paid Secretary his salary to Oct. 1, 1856, ...	$1,500 00	
Paid Secretary for clerk hire to Oct. 1, 1856, ...	635 00	
Paid Treasurer for State Farm improvements, . . .	3,000 00	
Paid expenses of the Secretary,	250 50	
" " " members of the board, ...	915 47	
Paid books and binding, . .	366 23	
		6,667 20

Military.

Adjutant and Quartermaster-General's Department. Resolve 1856, ch. 16.
Paid as per Resolve, ... \ . . $4,550 00

Militia Bounty. Act 1849, ch. 218. Act 1852, ch. 104.; 1853, ch. 174. Resolve 1855, ch. 65.
Paid, ... 52,888 00

Military Accounts.
Paid, per Rev. Stat., § 12, and Act 1852, ch. 104, ... 5,832 53

Armories. Act 1853, ch. 188.
Paid the several cities and towns rents to January 1, 1856, ... 11,877 31

Reformatory and Correctional.

County Treasurers. Rev. Stat., ch. 141, Act 1841, ch. 74.
Paid two-thirds of criminal costs, as per bills rendered, ... $135,134 45

Arrest of Fugitives from Justice. Rev. Stat., ch. 142.
Paid under Executive warrants, . . . 1,552 98

Expenses State Reform School for Boys. Resolves 1855, ch. 67, and 1856, ch. 91.
Paid to Treasurer of the board of trustees for support of inmates, ... 40,390 00

Expenses Industrial School for Girls. Resolves 1856, ch. 26 and 56.
Paid to the Commissioners for
the purchase of furniture, . $5,000 00
Paid to the Trustees for furnishing supplies, ... 8,000 00
—————
13,000 00

Agent for Discharged Convicts. Act 1852,
　　ch. 213.
Paid to Agent for salary and expenses to Oct.
　1, 1856, ... $1,000 00

Prevention of Counterfeiting, Resolve 1852,
　　ch. 76.
Paid to the Treasurer of the association, .   2,500 00

Public Buildings, not provided for by Scrip.

State House Enlargement. Resolve 1855,
　　ch. 59, Resolve 1854, ch. 452, § 4 ; Re-
　　solves 1856, ch. 12, 36.
Paid for materials and labor, ... $7,349 77

State Prison. Resolve 1856, ch. 81.
Paid for new boilers and setting
　the same, ... $3,000 00
Paid for raising the wall around
　the prison, three feet, &c., .   6,000 00
Paid for replenishing the library,   200 00
　　　　　　　　　　　　　　　　　　——————
　　　　　　　　　　　　　　　　　　 9,200 00

Taunton Lunatic Hospital. Rev. Stat., ch.
　　48, § 2, and Resolve 1855, ch. 66.
Paid for materials and labor, ...   9,846 13

Industrial School for Girls. Act 1855, ch.
　　442, Resolve 1855, ch. 83.
Paid for materials and labor, ...   21,802 13

State Almshouses. Resolves 1855, ch. 76,
　　78. Resolve 1856, ch. 54, 49, 94.
Paid for materials and labor, ...   32,000 62

Interest.

On Temporary Loans, . . $50,347 19
On scrip 1849, . . $5,000 00
　"　"　1850, . . 5,000 00
　"　"　1852, . . 9,750 00
　"　"　1853, . . 9,925 00

On scrip 1854, . $14,375 00
On scrip 1856, .   . 8,100 00
Western Railroad,   . 49,725 00
                      ——————— . $101,875 00
                                              $152,222 19
Sundry accounts, ...   34 31

    Total Ordinary Expenditures, .   .   . $1,335,096 45

    Temporary Loans repaid.
Loans of 1854, 1855 and 1856,   .   .   .   665,652 80

    Massachusetts School Fund.
Amount paid for securities purchased,   .   .   28,000 00

    Interest on School Fund.
Paid for educational expenses, as
  per Act 1854, ch. 300, .   . $47,215 57
Paid to the several towns, as per
  Act 1854, ch. 300,   .   .   44,842 95
Paid to the several towns, as per
  Resolve 1856, ch. 37 and 55,   179 55
Paid to the several towns, as per
  Resolve 1856, ch. 19, 21, and 24,   199 54
Paid Massachusetts School Fund,   1,534 97
  "   "   "   "   234 09
                                                94,206 67

    Interest on School Fund for Indians.
Amount paid as per Act 1837, ch. 85,   .   .   150 00

    School Fund for Indians.
Amount paid for securities purchased, .   .   2,500 00

    Todd Normal School Fund.
Amount paid for securities purchased, .   .   1,100 00

    Interest on Todd Normal School Fund.
Paid Treasurer of the Board of Education, .   714 00

    Western Railroad Stock Sinking Fund.
Paid for securities purchased,   .   .   .   77,400 00

State Almshouse Loan Sinking Fund.
Paid for securities purchased,   .   .   . $9,000 00

Western Railroad Loan Sinking Fund.
Paid the Commissioners, ...   40,000 00

Charles River and Warren Bridge Fund.
        Act 1854, ch. 451.
Paid Commissioners,   .   . $367 60
Paid for land taken to widen the
    bridge, ...   6,123 85
Paid on account of repairs and
    labor, ...   81,330 49
                                              —————
                                                         87,821 94

Industrial School for Girls.   Act 1855, ch.
        442, and Resolve 1855, ch. 83.
Paid on account of the above,   .   .   .   462 82

Northampton Lunatic Hospital.
Paid on account of building, ...   113,159 62

Interest on Railroad Scrip.
Andover and Haverhill,   .   . $4,825 00
Boston and Portland,   .   .   2,500 00
Eastern, ...   25,150 00
Norwich and Worcester, .   .   20,200 00
                                              —————
                                                         52,675 00

Hassanamessett Indian Fund.
Amount of interest paid for two years,   .   .   16 24
                                              —————————
                                                         $1,172,859 09
    Ordinary Expenditures before stated,   .   1,335,096 45
                                              —————————
                                                         $2,507,955 54

Cash on hand January 1, 1857.
On account of interest on School
    Fund for Indians, .   .   . $75 00
Hassanamessett Indian Fund,   .   162 50
Charles River and Warren Bridge
    Fund, ...   2,301 68   .

Interest on Todd Normal School Fund, ...	$1 45	
Income of Mass. School Fund,	20,349 83	
Western Railroad Stock Sinking Fund, ...	8,028 20	
Massachusetts School Fund, .	1,053 00	
State Almshouse Loan Sinking Fund, ...	1,609 29	
Andover and Haverhill Railroad,	1,300 00	
Norwich and Worcester Railroad,	10,500 00	
Eastern Railroad, . . .	3,100 00	
Cash on hand, borrowed in anticipation of the revenue, and the sale of scrip, . . .	96,362 30	
		$144,843 25
		$2,652,798 79

RECEIPTS AND EXPENDITURES

FROM 1850 TO 1856.

An Analysis of Receipts and Expenditures from 1850 to 1856, inclusive, appended to the Report of the Auditor for the year ending December 31, 1856.

RECEIPTS.	1850.	1851.	1852.	1853.	1854.	1855.	1856.
ORDINARY REVENUE.							
Bank Tax,	$354,742 22	$391,066 26	$430,260 77	$443,340 00	$525,867 87	$578,983 30	$583,445 43
State Tax,	–	–	–	286,605 00	279,150 00	428,108 00	584,884 45
Auction Tax,	12,958 93	14,759 49	12,026 22	85 86	–	–	–
Per cent. on State Tax,	–	–	–	–	–	–	798 13
Insurance Tax,	–	206 24	1,344 33	5,082 54	4,231 61	1,258 15	3,312 13
Alien Passengers,	35,136 08	37,066 54	29,459 52	31,008 51	52,634 73	15,848 62	16,878 68
Hawkers and Peddlers,	2,082 00	2,018 00	963 00	542 00	528 00	–	521 00
Attorney for Suffolk County,	4,131 80	6,122 74	3,385 86	4,709 70	4,633 15	3,719 40	529 97
Alien Estates,	251 54	3,179 53	237 14	2,515 82	705 01	773 15	966 77
Income West'n R.R. Stock Sink'g Fund,	–	28,540 92	36,658 23	35,951 21	62,488 82	61,897 00	52,870 99
Western Railroad Dividends,	80,000 00	80,000 00	75,000 00	65,000 00	59,696 00	49,392 00	49,392 00
Interest on deposits,	521 61	1,076 30	1,428 75	1,861 82	1,276 45	792 48	1,620 69
Premium on Scrip sold,	500 00	340 00	4,520 00	4,172 50	1,060 00	200 00	7,633 50
Bank Penalties,	–	–	–	–	1,500 00	2,000 00	–
Accrued interest on Scrip sold,	1,870 28	1,940 96	1,319 44	1,204 86	2,403 38	4,603 06	11,178 17
Commissioner of Insolvency,	86 50	80 16	–	–	–	–	–
Sundry accounts,	529 68	34 95	1,567 23	209 50	–	241 04	14,773 88
Total, Ordinary Revenue,	$492,810 64	$566,432 09	$598,170 49	$882,289 32	$996,175 02	$1,147,816 20	$1328,805 79
EXTRAORDINARY REVENUE.							
Temporary Loan,	$495,600 00	$345,000 00	$550,000 00	$546,800 00	$617,437 00	$740,584 95	$400,315 80
Scrip sold,	125,000 00	150,000 00	200,000 00	175,000 00	120,000 00	74,000 00	370,000 00
Massachusetts School Fund,	76,246 00	248,786 73	99,047 75	239,659 07	95,047 32	46,795 92	27,127 16
Income Massachusetts School Fund,	39,972 53	46,259 11	44,147 56	49,078 32	85,695 24	89,637 18	84,627 49

Income School Fund for Indians,	150 00	150 00	150 00	150 00	150 00	150 00	225 00
Todd Normal School Fund,	10,797 72	–	11,509 44	1,100 00	–	–	1,100 00
Interest Todd Normal School Fund,	248 95	539 88	–	829 28	714 00	714 00	715 45
Hassanamessett Indian Fund,	279 00	46 00	–	44 66	21 00	–	16 24
Charles River & Warren Bridge Fund,	4,284 55	5,078 55	6,378 49	7,727 39	59,446 60	100,474 50	90,123 62
Western R. R. Loan Sinking Fund,	40,000 00	40,000 00	40,000 00	40,000 00	40,000 00	40,000 00	40,000 00
Western R. R. Stock Sinking Fund,	143,871 63	47,619 95	97,947 75	123,027 13	74,333 37	81,348 93	85,124 92
Almshouse Sinking Fund,	–	–	–	3,075 00	9,204 75	6,484 50	9,920 04
Subscription to Reform School for Girls,	–	–	–	–	–	17,550 00	2,575 00
Interest on—							
Andover and Haverhill R. R. Scrip,	5,000 00	5,000 00	5,000 00	5,000 00	5,000 00	5,000 00	5,000 00
Boston and Portland R. R. Scrip,	2,500 00	2,500 00	2,500 00	2,500 00	2,500 00	2,500 00	2,500 00
Eastern Railroad Scrip,	25,000 00	25,000 00	25,000 00	25,000 00	27,500 00	25,000 00	25,000 00
Norwich and Worcester R. R. Scrip,	20,000 00	20,000 00	20,000 00	20,000 00	10,000 00	30,000 00	20,000 00
Premium on Scrip sold,	–	–	5,030 00	–	940 00	–	–
State House, (sundries sold,)	–	–	–	–	159 07	149 81	–
Over allowance on Educational Expen's	–	–	–	–	–	11 00	–
School Fund for Indians,	–	–	–	–	–	–	2,500 00
Total, Extraordinary Revenue,	$988,950 38	$935,980 22	$1,106,710 99	$1,238,990 75	$1,148,148 35	$1,210,400 79	$1,166,870 72

EXPENDITURES—ORDINARY REVENUE.	1850.	1851.	1852.	1853.	1854.	1855.	1856.
LEGISLATIVE AND EXECUTIVE.							
Council,	$4,918 00	$5,153 00	$5,481 00	$6,104 00	$7,303 00	$8,158 00	$10,339 00
Legislature,	90,912 00	139,469 20	134,330 20	105,288 50	139,038 61	197,911 77	199,155 53
Salaries,	76,108 66	78,267 94	81,138 87	84,996 43	92,191 02	100,432 39	114,854 94
Fuel and Lights,	1,231 61	1,128 53	1,063 30	1,124 43	1,300 00	3,000 00	2,647 97
Repairs,	4,486 29	3,147 08	3,125 18	5,836 22	13,851 27	13,502 80	16,615 69
Furniture,	283 52	1,742 77	1,760 37	1,105 13	1,916 16	2,447 01	8,113 94
Stationery,	2,255 40	3,062 41	4,485 39	3,429 71	4,398 58	8,899 93	8,744 73
State Library,	600 00	300 00	300 00	804 13	500 00	849 20	3,692 76
Newspapers,	3,847 32	5,861 09	5,767 98	6,123 38	5,947 46	9,026 18	8,854 61
Printing,	19,465 05	20,876 26	25,168 80	27,009 14	31,142 08	53,520 89	47,616 28
Postage,	626 43	624 83	462 97	695 98	956 47	1,379 50	1,583 87
Index and Journals,	1,347 00	264 00	680 00	5,119 37	17,754 51	28,747 63	19,196 10
Sheriffs,	926 58	1,264 83	724 93	1,322 57	655 64	791 87	736 60
Contingent Fund,	1,000 00	2,000 00	2,000 00	2,000 00	2,000 00	2,500 00	2,500 00
International Exchange,	300 00	300 00	300 00	—	600 00	—	—
Documents in London,	304 25	213 74	237 61	—	—	—	—
Bank Commissioners,	3,668 60	3,156 15	4,889 00	5,574 70	6,793 10	5,378 25	6,983 85
Commissioners—various purposes,	4,802 05	7,134 54	3,741 87	6,663 22	10,283 86	14,568 09	4,446 89
Indemnification of Officers,	—	—	—	—	—	—	8,322 84
Term Reports,	1,867 25	3,055 65	2,616 35	2,518 00	962 50	1,542 57	2,214 10
Valuation Committee,	125 29	13,885 50	—	—	—	—	—
Legal Counsel,	1,500 00	—	—	1,862 27	115 70	50 00	300 00
Miscellaneous,	2,515 90	7,478 18	2,391 15	2,325 29	1,399 75	10,507 39	—
Alien Estates reclaimed,	939 89	—	96 85	—	—	—	—
Annuity to Harvard College,	666 66	666 66	666 66	666 66	666 66	666 66	666 66
Weights, Measures and Balances,	—	750 00	—	600 00	450 00	300 00	157 00
Land Office,	—	—	—	—	403 61	1,000 30	1,000 00

Insurance Commissioners,	—	—	—	—	366 06	5,401 51	7,284 40
Courts of Insolvency,	—	—	—	—	—	—	7,124 43
Presidential Electors,	—	—	—	—	—	—	233 60
Census and Statistics,	—	—	—	—	—	—	32,350 34
Convention of 1853,	—	—	—	154,184 82	11,205 16	345 25	—
Reception of Kossuth,	—	—	11,591 38	93 10	—	—	—
Reception of President,	—	7,227 22	506 00	—	—	—	—
Secret Ballot,	—	1,806 36	710 68	1,542 47	—	—	—
Totals, Legislative and Executive,	$224,697 75	$308,835 94	$294,236 54	$426,989 52	$352,201 20	$470,927 19	$515,736 13
CHARITABLE.							
Asylum for Blind,	$14,000 00	$9,000 00	$9,000 00	$9,000 00	$9,000 00	$10,500 00	$12,000 00
School for Idiots,	2,500 00	3,750 00	3,750 00	5,000 00	5,000 00	30,000 00	5,000 00
Asylum for Deaf and Dumb,	8,205 58	7,892 05	9,726 96	7,567 41	7,309 24	7,752 77	8,909 33
Eye and Ear Infirmary,	7,000 00	2,000 00	2,000 00	2,500 00	2,500 00	2,500 00	2,500 00
Expenses Taunton Hospital,	—	—	—	—	11,785 08	2,706 94	3,070 98
Expenses Worcester Hospital,	3,200 00	3,200 00	3,200 00	3,200 00	3,200 00	3,200 00	2,775 00
Annuity Martha Johonnot,	2,212 82	2,140 00	2,148 33	2,040 00	1,971 38	1,910 11	1,640 00
State Paupers,	112,265 35	107,515 63	100,647 72	103,330 43	100,730 93	86,854 09	66,878 06
Expenses State Almshouses,	—	—	—	—	80,900 61	172,558 80	173,565 13
Coroners' account,	2,773 44	1,607 14	2,754 00	1,962 55	2,002 69	2,388 56	1,959 36
Indians,	—	3,919 86	2,190 91	1,880 96	1,547 40	3,066 63	2,654 60
Pensioners,	1,552 67	1,474 26	1,112 55	855 64	731 04	827 50	1,370 20
Alien Commissioners,	—	2,670 16	8,230 89	8,543 80	7,958 22	9,634 24	11,237 08
Alien Passengers,	150 00	—	—	3,025 00	6,750 00	6,000 00	6,000 00
Life Boats,	—	—	2,500 00	—	—	—	—
Totals, Charitable,	$153,859 86	$145,169 10	$147,261 36	$148,905 79	$241,386 59	$339,899 94	$299,559 74

An Analysis of Receipts and Expenditures—Continued.

EXPENDITURES—ORDINARY REVENUE.	1850.	1851.	1852.	1853.	1854.	1855.	1856.
SCIENTIFIC AND EDUCATIONAL.							
State Map and Survey,	$8 88	$25 00	$229 20	$114 23	$800 00	$54 80	$18 20
Agricultural Societies,	7,450 00	7,480 00	9,966 00	8,782 00	10,188 00	10,542 00	11,634 76
Board of Agriculture,	— —	— —	336 72	2,131 63	8,789 06	8,992 38	6,667 20
American Institute of Instruction,	— —	300 00	600 00	300 00	300 00	300 00	300 00
Bounty on Silk,	5 25	— —	— —	— —	— —	— —	— —
Totals, Scientific and Educational,	$7,464 13	$7,805 00	$11,131 92	$11,327 86	$20,077 06	$19,889 18	$18,620 16
MILITARY.							
Adjutant and Q'r-Master General's Dep.,	$3,000 00	$4,650 00	$2,893 00	$3,350 00	$5,800 00	$4,550 00	$4,550 00
Militia Bounty,	22,552 50	23,843 50	25,569 00	29,098 50	53,488 25	54,419 00	52,888 00
Military Accounts,	1,272 36	1,126 61	1,191 74	4,113 14	2,910 60	7,090 48	5,832 53
Rent of Armories,	— —	— —	— —	— —	6,427 82	12,280 00	11,877 31
Totals, Military,	$26,824 86	$29,620 11	$29,653 74	$36,561 64	$68,626 67	$78,339 48	$75,147 84
REFORMATORY AND CORRECTIONAL.							
County Treasurer,	$69,947 05	$53,199 44	$86,268 90	$99,094 57	$110,885 29	$182,235 50	$135,134 45
Arrest of Fugitives,	189 87	946 20	1,115 50	859 22	2,812 08	1,403 64	1,552 98
Reform School Expenses,	22,600 00	22,500 00	20,000 00	30,000 00	45,200 00	47,960 00	40,390 00
Industrial School Expenses,	— —	— —	— —	— —	— —	— —	13,000 00
Agent for Discharged Convicts,	650 00	700 00	618 45	1,000 00	1,000 00	1,000 00	1,000 00
Prevention of Counterfeiting,	1,169 35	965 96	435 60	1,079 37	3,530 37	2,500 00	2,500 00
Bank Penalty refunded,	— —	— —	— —	— —	— —	3,500 00	— —
State Prison Expenses,	— —	— —	1,320 00	— —	— —	— —	— —
Totals, Reformatory and Correct'l,	$94,556 27	$78,311 60	$109,758 45	$132,033 16	$163,427 74	$238,599 14	$193,577 43

INTEREST.							
On Temporary Loan,	$7,082 65	$5,266 68	$4,820 27	$6,669 72	$20,170 36	$23,125 48	$50,347 19
On Western Railroad Scrip,	49,750 00	48,950 00	50,025 00	50,100 00	49,500 00	50,050 00	49,725 00
On State Scrip,	1,250 00	10,000 00	17,500 00	24,425 00	29,400 00	39,975 00	52,150 00
Accrued for West'n R.R. Stock S. Fund,	—	147 00	—	—	243 17	—	—
Totals, Interest,	$58,082 65	$64,363 68	$72,345 27	$81,194 72	$99,313 53	$113,150 48	$152,222 19
PUBLIC BUILDINGS, &c.							
State Prison,	$570 00	$8,000 00	$9,699 76	$40,551 01	$5,000 00	$16,415 49	$9,200 00
Malden Bridge,	—	—	—	—	9,000 00	—	—
Charles River and Warren Bridge,	—	—	—	—	5,171 40	4,358 85	—
State Almshouses,	—	—	—	—	26,756 94	50,870 67	32,000 62
State House Enlargement,	—	—	—	—	—	70,754 09	7,349 77
Taunton Hospital,	—	—	—	—	—	8,001 07	9,846 13
Industrial School,	—	—	—	—	—	—	21,802 13
Totals, Public Buildings, &c.,	$570 00	$8,000 00	$9,699 76	$40,551 01	$45,928 34	$150,400 17	$80,198 65
Sundry accounts,	—	—	$535 33	—	$14 86	$32 04	$34 31

An Analysis of Receipts and Expenditures—Continued.

.PAYMENTS EXTRAORDINARY.	1850.	1851.	1852.	1853.	1854.	1855.	1856.
Temporary Loan,	$495,600 00	$365,000 00	$475,000 00	$446,800 00	$482,500 00	$433,184 95	$665,652 80
State Prison Enlargement,	46,457 32	42,085 17	11,457 51	– –	78,000 00	– –	– –
Massachusetts School Fund,	56,103 10	277,569 04	79,515 74	250,268 04	113,134 51	45,500 00	28,000 00
Income School Fund,	37,060 66	43,943 09	45,602 53	48,892 99	72,403 17	94,162 79	94,206 67
Interest on School Fund for Indians,	150 00	150 00	150 00	150 00	150 00	150 00	150 00
Western R.R. Stock Sinking Fund,	106,682 50	81,661 00	40,900 00	154,400 00	106,100 00	31,300 00	77,400 00
Western R.R. Loan Sinking Fund,	40,000 00	40,000 00	40,000 00	40,000 00	40,000 00	40,000 00	40,000 00
Charles River and Warren Bridges,	6,050 00	5,400 00	5,004 70	7,086 27	62,228 97	100,474 50	87,821 94
Todd Normal School Fund,	11,046 67	– –	11,509 44	1,100 00	– –	– –	1,100 00
Andover and Haverhill Railroad,	5,275 00	4,600 00	5,050 00	4,975 00	5,200 00	5,325 00	4,825 00
Boston and Portland Railroad,	2,500 00	2,500 00	2,500 00	2,500 00	2,500 00	2,500 00	2,500 00
Eastern Railroad,	23,600 00	23,535 00	23,600 00	28,925 00	24,600 00	25,675 00	25,150 00
Norwich and Worcester Railroad,	19,700 00	20,550 00	20,025 00	19,950 00	19,350 00	20,325 00	20,200 00
Interest on Todd Normal School Fund,	– –	539 88	– –	829 28	714 00	714 00	714 00
Taunton Lunatic Hospital,	– –	– –	60,364 24	58,228 45	66,542 55	864 76	– –
State Almshouses,	– –	– –	20,257 74	94,255 37	100,488 14	– –	– –
Loan of 1851, paid,	– –	– –	– –	100,000 00	– –	– –	– –
Hassanamessett Indian Fund,	– –	– –	– –	169 66	58 50	– –	16 24
Enlargement State House,	– –	– –	– –	48,361 19	84,915 82	32,031 87	– –
Almshouse Sinking Fund,	– –	– –	– –	– –	12,075 00	6,000 00	9,000 00
Reform School for Girls,	– –	– –	– –	– –	– –	19,662 18	462 82
Northampton Lunatic Hospital,	– –	– –	– –	– –	– –	17,343 42	113,159 62
School Fund for Indians,	– –	– –	– –	– –	– –	– –	2,500 00
Totals, Payments Extraordinary,	$850,225 25	$907,523 18	$840,936 90	$1,306,891 25	$1,270,960 66	$875,213 47	$1,172,859 09

RECAPITULATION.

	1850.	1851.	1852.	1853.	1854.	1855.	1856.
RECEIPTS.							
Ordinary Revenue,	$492,810 64	$566,482 09	$598,170 49	$882,289 32	$996,175 02	$1,147,816 20	$1,328,805 79
Extraordinary Revenue,	988,950 38	935,980 22	1,106,710 99	1,238,990 75	1,148,148 35	1,210,400 79	1,166,870 72
Total, Receipts,	$1,481,761 02	$1,502,412 31	$1,704,881 48	$2,121,280 07	$2,144,323 37	$2,358,216 99	$2,495,676 51
PAYMENTS—ORDINARY.							
Legislative and Executive,	$224,697 75	$308,835 94	$294,236 54	$426,989 52	$352,201 20	$470,927 19	$515,736 13
Charitable,	153,859 86	145,169 10	147,261 36	148,905 79	241,386 59	339,899 94	299,559 74
Scientific and Educational,	7,464 13	7,805 00	11,131 92	11,327 86	20,077 06	19,899 18	18,620 16
Military,	26,824 86	29,620 11	29,658 74	36,561 64	68,626 67	78,339 48	75,147 84
Reformatory and Correctional,	94,556 27	78,311 60	109,758 45	132,033 16	163,427 74	238,599 14	193,577 43
Interest,	58,082 65	64,363 68	72,345 27	81,194 72	99,313 53	113,150 48	152,222 19
Public Buildings, &c.,	570 00	8,000 00	9,699 76	40,551 01	45,928 34	150,400 17	80,198 65
Sundry accounts,	— —	— —	535 33	— —	14 86	32 04	34 31
Total, Ordinary Expenditures,	$566,055 54	$642,105 41	$674,622 37	$877,563 70	$990,975 99	$1,411,237 62	$1,335,096 45
Total, Extraordinary Expenditures,	850,225 25	907,523 18	840,936 90	1,306,891 25	1,270,960 66	875,213 47	1,172,859 09
Grand Totals,	$1,416,280 79	$1,549,628 59	$1,515,559 27	$2,184,454 95	$2,261,936 65	$2,286,451 09	$2,507,955 54

ESTIMATED RECEIPTS AND EXPENDITURES FOR THE YEAR 1857, IN DETAIL, ON ACCOUNT OF ORDINARY REVENUE.

RECEIPTS.

Bank Tax, ...	$585,000 00
State Tax, (remaining unpaid Jan. 1, 1857,) .	71,216 05
Insurance Tax, ...	2,000 00
Alien Estates, ...	1,000 00
Alien Passengers, ...	15,000 00
Income Western Railroad Stock Sinking Fund,	30,000 00
Western Railroad dividends, ...	49,000 00
Interest on deposits, ...	1,000 00
Hawkers and Peddlers, ...	500 00
Courts of Insolvency, ...	12,000 00
Salaries, fees received by the Secretary of State,	1,000 00
Total estimated receipts for 1857, . .	$767,716 05

EXPENDITURES.

Legislative and Executive.

Council, ...	$10,000 00
Legislature, ...	180,000 00
Salaries, ...	120,000 00
Fuel and Lights, . . .	3,000 00
Repairs upon the State House, .	6,000 00
Furniture, (including bills of 1855 and 6, remaining unpaid,) .	4,000 00
Stationery, ...	8,000 00
State Library, ...	1,000 00
Newspapers and Advertising, .	9,000 00
State Printing, ...	50,000 00
Postage, ...	1,500 00
Index and Journals, . . .	25,000 00

Sheriffs, ...	$800 00	
Contingent Fund, . . .	2,500 00	
Bank Commissioners, . .	7,000 00	
Insurance Commissioners, .	7,000 00	
Commissioners for various purposes, (including Com. for Rev. Statutes,)	10,000 00	
Indemnification of Officers, .	5,000 00	
Term Reports, ...	2,000 00	
Weights and Measures for towns,	500 00	
Land Office, ...	1,000 00	
Courts of Insolvency, . .	34,000 00	
		$487,300 00

Educational and Scientific.

State Map and Survey, . .	$50 00	
State Board of Agriculture, .	8,000 00	
Agricultural Societies, . .	12,000 00	
American Institute of Instruction,	300 00	
		$20,350 00

Charitable.

Asylum for the Blind, . .	$12,000 00
School for Idiots, . . .	5,000 00
Asylum for the Deaf and Dumb,	9,000 00
Eye and Ear Infirmary, . .	2,500 00
Expenses Taunton Lunatic Hospital, ...	3,200 00
Expenses Worcester Lunatic Hospital, ...	3,200 00
Annuities of Martha Johonnott,	2,000 00
State Paupers, including Lunatics,	75,000 00
Expenses of the four State Almshouses, ...	170,000 00
Coroners, ...	2,500 00
Indians, ...	3,000 00
Pensioners, ...	1,200 00
Alien Commissioners, including Agents employed, . . .	10,000 00

Alien Passengers, (amount to be carried to State Almshouse Fund,)	$6,000 00	
Expenses Northampton Lunatic Hospital, ...	1,000 00	
		$305,600 00

Military.

Adjutant and Quartermaster-General's Department, . .	$5,000 00	
Militia Bounty, ...	53,000 00	
Military Accounts, . . .	6,000 00	
Rent of Armories, . . .	12,000 00	
		$76,000 00

Reformatory and Correctional.

County Treasurers, . . .	$200,000 00	
Arrest of Fugitives, . . .	2,000 00	
Expenses of the Reform School for Boys, ...	42,960 00	
Expenses of the Industrial School for Girls, ...	13,500 00	
Agents for Discharged Convicts,	1,000 00	
		$259,460 00

Interest.

Temporary Loans, . . .	$25,000 00	
State Scrip, 5 and 6 per cent., .	65,000 00	
Western Railroad Scrip, . .	50,000 00	
		$140,000 00
		$1,288,710 00

WESTERN RAILROAD LOAN SINKING FUND.

This Fund was created with the Albany Sinking Fund, to secure the payment of $4,000,000 of scrip loaned by the Commonwealth at 5 per cent., and $1,000,000 loaned by the city of Albany at 6 per cent., making about one-half the cost of the road. These funds now amount to $1,640,507.87.

The Commonwealth now holds 7,056 shares Western Railroad Stock, exclusive of those in the School and Stock Sinking .Funds.

These shares will be entitled to their proportion of the Loan Sinking Fund, now worth $32.14 per share, or $226,779.84 on the whole. The amount of increase during the year has been $2.77 per share.

Schedule of Stocks and Securities in the Treasury, belonging to the Commonwealth, January 1, 1857.

Western Railroad Stock,	$705,600 00	
Western R. R. Stock in Sch'l Fund,	376,500 00	
Western Railroad Stock in Stock Sinking Fund, . . .	94,300 00	
		$1,176,400 00
Massachusetts 5 per cent. Scrip in School and Sinking Fund, ...		255,000 00
Railroad Scrip 5 per cent. in School and Sinking Funds, ...		384,000 00
State of Maine 5 per cent. Scrip in School and Sinking Funds, . . : . . .		250,000 00
Notes for lands in Maine, in School and Sinking Funds, ...		255,881 74
County, City, and Town Scrip, in the various funds, ...		459,370 00
Notes and Mortgages in the various funds, .		282,935 23
Notes, with collateral and with sureties, . .		265,000 00
		$3,328,586 97
Rights in the Western Railroad Sinking Fund, present value, ...		378,197 36
		$3,706,784 33
Amount, January 1, 1856, . . .		3,673,340 16
Increase, ...		$33,444 17

There is due and unpaid of land notes—

Principal, ...		$137,219 58
Interest, due January 1, 1857, . . .		37,292 44

Schedule of Securities in the Western Railroad Loan Sinking Fund, belonging to the Corporation, and in charge of the Treasurer of the Commonwealth.

Notes and Mortgages,	$394,041 91
Notes and collateral,	177,544 25
Boston and Providence Railroad Stock,	14,437 00
Boston and Worcester Railroad Stock,	35,953 23
Boston and Lowell Railroad Stock,	26,298 75
Pittsfield and North Adams Railroad Stock,	20,045 50
Massachusetts sterling Scrip,	5,760 00
Boston and Worcester Railroad Bonds,	221,000 00
Connecticut River Railroad Bonds,	200,000 00
...ord and New Haven Railroad Bonds,	47,500 00
	302 30

Reformu....

		$1,142,882 94
County Treasurers,	$200,...	18,791 18
Arrest of Fugitives,	2,000	
		$1,161,674 12
Expenses of the Reform School for Boys,	42,960 00	
Expenses of the Industrial School for Girls,	13,500 00	328,586 97
Agents for Discharged Convicts,	1,000 00	'61 09
		$259,460

·ear,

Interest.

Temporary Loans,	$25,000 00	
State Scrip, 5 and 6 per cent.,	65,000 00	
Western Railroad Scrip,	50,000 00	
		$140,000 00
		$1,288,710 00

WESTERN RAILROAD LOAN SINKING FUND.

This Fund was created with the Albany Sinking Fund, to secure the payment of $4,000,000 of scrip loaned by the Commonwealth at 5 per cent., and $1,000,000 loaned by the city of Albany at 6 per cent., making about one-half the cost of the road. These funds now amount to $1,640,507.87.

previous year, in consequence of charters having been granted
by the legislature of 1856.

The receipts for Insurance Tax for the year 1856, was
$3,312.13. This sum is paid by the foreign insurance compa-
nies doing business within the Commonwealth. The receipts
from this source are very fluctuating, therefore the estimate for
1857 is for $2,000.

While the receipts from Alien Passengers amount to
$16,878.68, during 1856, yet so large a sum cannot be relied
upon for the year to come,—a circumstance which cannot be
regretted, as the larger portion of that class of emigrants who
pay this bounty, ultimately become an expense and burden upon
the State. The estimated receipts from this source for 1857,
are $15,000.

The amount received from Public Administrators on account
of Alien Estates, in 1856, was $965.87. The estimate for 1857
is $1,000.

The sum paid into the treasury by the Attorney of Suffolk
County, received by him for forfeited recognizances in 1856,
was $529.97. By the Act of 1855, chapter 449, the income
from this source is paid to the City of Boston, thus decreasing
the State revenue from $4,000 to $5,000 a year.

The revenue from the Courts of Insolvency for 1856, amounting to $195, was received for the quarter ending September 30,
which is no criterion for the future. I have estimated the re-
would conduct his own affairs.
for 1857, or $8,000, is based upon the actual cost in 1855 and 6.

The expenses for Fuel and Lights, which cost in 1856,
$2,647.97, would be reduced nearly one-half, or from ten to
twelve hundred dollars a year. The estimate for 1857, is $3,000.

The expenses of Newspapers is also dependent, in no small
degree, upon the length of the session. The amount paid in
1856, was $8,854.61. It is believed that this item could, with
great propriety, be reduced some five thousand dollars annually.

When it is taken into consideration that the expenses of our
Commonwealth exceed those of the combined States of Maine,
New Hampshire, Vermont, Rhode Island and Connecticut,
would it not be a profitable subject for the present legislature
to consider, whether a reform could not be advantageously
introduced in our own State.

The amount of interest received for money deposited during the year 1856, was $1,620.69, a much larger sum than usual. The estimate for 1857 is $1,000.

The receipts on account of the Charles River and Warren Bridges, amounting to $9,530.25, were for money advanced previous to January 1, 1856.

The per cent. on State Tax, received during the year 1856, amounting to $798.13, was on account of delinquency of sundry towns to pay their tax within the time specified by law.

The sum received on account of State Printing, amounting to $2,533.44, was on account of printing done for the Board of Education, during the year 1855, and which should properly come out of the School Fund.

The amount received under the head of Sundry Accounts, of $271.57, was for over-allowances refunded on account of Arrest of Fugitives, Militia, Census and Statistics, Sheriffs and Paupers.

The income from the Western Railroad Stock Sinking Fund, during the year 1856, amounted to $52,870.99. The estimated receipts from this source, of $30,000 in 1857, is up to the 15th of July, when the payment of the bonds are to be made.

The Western Railroad dividends amounted in 1856 to $49,392, it being 7 per cent. on 7,056 shares held by the Commonwealth. The estimate for 1857 is about the same, $49,000.

The receipts from premium and accrued interest on scrip sold, amounted during the year 1856, to $18,811.67.

ear,

Interest.

Temporary Loans, . . .	$25,000	00
State Scrip, 5 and 6 per cent., .	65,000	00
Western Railroad Scrip, . .	50,000	00
	$140,000	00
	$1,288,710	00

WESTERN RAILROAD LOAN SINKING FUND.

This Fund was created with the Albany Sinking Fund, to secure the payment of $4,000,000 of scrip loaned by the Commonwealth at 5 per cent., and $1,000,000 loaned by the city of Albany at 6 per cent., making about one-half the cost of the road. These funds now amount to $1,640,507.87.

Notwithstanding the resources of our State are at present immense, and amply sufficient to meet any demands that may be made upon them, yet it would seem that the time had arrived when some measures adequate to the emergency should be devised, to prevent, if possible, the great increase of State expenses, and consequently lessen the direct taxation which has heretofore been found necessary, in order to meet the great and increasing expenditures; otherwise the financial credit of our Commonwealth may eventually be placed in a no less enviable position than that of some of our sister States of the Union. Is it not, therefore, highly desirable, in view of the present expenditures of our State, that some means should be resorted to by which they may be reduced?

The items of the " Legislative and Executive " expenses have rapidly increased within the past few years, one of considerable expense, amounting in 1856, to $8,744.73. It is believed that the quantity heretofore consumed has been double what is really required for consumption in the public business. This extravagance is chargeable, in a great measure, upon the clerks, who have it under their immediate control.

1853,	6,369	12
1854,	9,125	57
1855,	11,338	22

My own convictions are that the public business, in all its departments, should be conducted upon the same principles of justice and economy that every prudent individual would conduct his own affairs.

for 1857, of $3,000, is based upon the actual cost in 1855 and 6.

The expenses for Fuel and Lights, which cost in 1856, $2,647.97, would be reduced nearly one-half, or from ten to twelve hundred dollars a year. The estimate for 1857, is $3,000.

The expenses of Newspapers is also dependent, in no small degree, upon the length of the session. The amount paid in 1856, was $8,854.61. It is believed that this item could, with great propriety, be reduced some five thousand dollars annually.

When it is taken into consideration that the expenses of our Commonwealth exceed those of the combined States of Maine, New Hampshire, Vermont, Rhode Island and Connecticut, would it not be a profitable subject for the present legislature to consider, whether a reform could not be advantageously introduced in our own State.

Legislative and Executive.

Under this head are included those accounts necessary for the expenses of the government, such as the Legislature, Executive Council, Salaries, Fuel and Lights, Repairs and Furniture for the State House, Stationery, Library, Newspapers and Advertising, State Printing, Postage, Indexes and Journals, Sheriffs' Accounts, Contingent Expenses, Bank, Insurance, and other Commissioners, Indemnification of Officers, Term Reports, Weights and Measures, Land Office, Annuity to Harvard College, Courts of Insolvency, Presidential Electors, Census and Statistics, and Legal Counsel, the cost of which for the year 1856, amounted to $515,736.13.

The expenses of the legislature have been, as is well known, ------------ amounting to $199,155.53 in 1856, and there of Fugitives, Militia, Census and Statistics, Sheriffs and Paupers.

The income from the Western Railroad Stock Sinking Fund, during the year 1856, amounted to $52,870.99. The estimated receipts from this source, of $30,000 in 1857, is up to the 15th of July, when the payment of the bonds are to be made.

The Western Railroad dividends amounted in 1856 to $49,392, it being 7 per cent. on 7,056 shares held by the Comber of the House of Representatives, either from ------ $40,000, quality or infrequency of representation, and of thus shortening the sessions, as has been so often suggested of late years, may ----- well to consider if the interests of the State would

Interest.

Temporary Loans, . . .	$25,000 00
State Scrip, 5 and 6 per cent., .	65,000 00
Western Railroad Scrip, . .	50,000 00
	—————
	$140,000
	—————
	$1,288,710 (

and fifty thousand dollars a year, but it would also reduce the expenses of several other departments, particularly those of the Executive Council, State Printing, Stationery, Fuel and Lights, Newspapers, Indexes and Journals, Postage, Salaries, and Contingent Expenses.

The expenses of the Executive Council, which amounted in

1856, to $10,339, would be reduced in proportion to that of the legislature, and there would be a saving of at least five thousand dollars a year, in this department. The estimate for 1857, is $10,000.

The cost of State Printing, amounting in 1856, to $47,616.28, has become quite an important item in the expenditures, and is enhanced by the length of the sessions. It might be reduced from twenty to thirty thousand dollars a year. The printing of the Daily Journal is a no inconsiderable item of the present expenditure, amounting to several thousand dollars each session. This is regarded by those most conversant with the subject, as almost entirely useless. In anticipation of the completion of the Plymouth Colony Records, during the present year, the estimate for Printing in 1857, is $50,000.

The item of Stationery has also become one of considerable expense, amounting in 1856, to $8,744.73. It is believed that the quantity heretofore consumed has been double what is really required for consumption in the public business. This extravagance is chargeable, in a great measure, upon the clerks, who have it under their immediate control. Th

1853,	6,369 12
1854,	9,125 57
1855,	11,338 22
1856,	18,825 69

proper and judicious management in this department a saving may be made of some four thousand dollars per annum. The estimate for 1857, of $8,000, is based upon the actual cost in 1855 and 6.

The expenses for Fuel and Lights, which cost in 1856, $2,647.97, would be reduced nearly one-half, or from ten to twelve hundred dollars a year. The estimate for 1857, is $3,000.

The expenses of Newspapers is also dependent, in no small degree, upon the length of the session. The amount paid in 1856, was $8,854.61. It is believed that this item could, with great propriety, be reduced some five thousand dollars annually. There can be no doubt that abuses have, and still do exist, in regard to this expenditure. The original intention unquestionably was, that each member should have, for his own private reading, newspapers of various political opinions, in order that he might the better become acquainted with the views of the people at large, have the proceedings of the previous day's session before him for perusal and reference, and thus become possessed of such general news and information as would enable him to perform his legislative duties understandingly, and thereby expedite the public business. The original design, however, has been greatly perverted. Some members have been known to take two, three, four, and even thirteen copies of the same paper: one for their own use, the remainder being mailed from the office of publication to friends in various parts of the country. Instances have been known where *eighteen copies of one periodical have been subscribed for by one member!* Periodicals, children's papers, and those devoted solely to literature are included in the lists thus subscribed for. It is sometimes the case that a private understanding is had with the publisher, and a charge is made to the State for several copies of each issue, while but one is delivered. Thus the actual time of subscription is made to extend to years after the person has ceased to be a member of the legislature. Custom appears to have sanctioned the same privileges to door-keepers, pages, and messengers in respect to newspapers, as are enjoyed by members of the legislature. It would seem to

[The following two paragraphs are printed overlapping on the page:]

The Western Railroad dividends amounted in 1856 to $49,392, it being 7 per cent. on 7,056 shares held by the Commonwealth. The estimate for 1857 is about the same, $49,000.

ber of the House of Representatives, either from the ... frequency of representation, and of thus shortening amount there was paid in 1856, $13,100.10. This expenditure, until the present year, has been mainly on account of the Massachusetts and Plymouth Colony Records. It would seem that this work had been prolonged to an unnecessary length of time, and some of those engaged upon it have not, in the opinion of many, labored with that assiduity which the public service demands. Would it not be well that measures should be taken, at the earliest moment, to finish the work already commenced, and guard against like unnecessary expenditures in the future? The estimate for 1857, is $25,000.

The item of Postage, which amounted to $1,583.87, in 1856, would be reduced nearly one-half. The estimate for 1857 is $1,500.

The Contingent Expenses are also dependent upon the duration of the sessions. The amount paid to the Sergeant-at-Arms on account of this fund in 1856, was $2,500, some ten or twelve hundred dollars of which might be saved yearly. The estimate for 1857 is $2,500.

The increase of salaries is, to some extent, chargeable to the same cause, particularly in the office of the Secretary of State, the expenses of which, for extra clerk hire, have increased nearly six fold within the past seven years, amounting, exclusive of the two permanent clerks, and the three clerks who are employed upon the Plymouth Records, to $18,825.69, for the year ending October 1, 1856. In my judgment the expenses of this department have been augmented to an unreasonable extent, and with a session of a reasonable length, might be reduced from ten to twelve thousand dollars a year. The following table will show at a glance the amounts paid for extra clerk hire in the Secretary's office, for each of the seven years past. The salary roll for 1856, amounted to $114,854.94. The estimate for 1857, is $120,000.

1850,	.	.	.	.	.	.	$3,685 00
1851,	.	.	.	.	.	.	5,439 75
1852,	.	.	.	.	.	.	5,518 76
1853,	.	.	.	.	.	.	6,369 12
1854,	.	.	.	.	.	.	9,125 57
1855,	.	.	.	.	.	.	11,338 22
1856,	.	.	.	.	.	.	18,825 69

The sum paid during the year 1856, for Furniture and Repairs, was $24,729.63, which exceeded the estimate of the Auditor of last year, $9,729.63.

Upon representations made to the legislature of 1856, that the Committee on Public Buildings for the previous year had overrun the appropriation for that year to a large amount, the sum of $17,172.80 was appropriated under the Resolve of 1856, chap. 32, for the payment of all such bills as were outstanding at that time. I learn, through the Sergeant-at-Arms, that that sum proved inadequate for the purpose to the amount of about $2,000. The legislature also appropriated, under the Resolve of 1856, chap. 98, $7,213, for repairs upon and about the State House, which sum has been drawn for. I am informed that the committee have again exceeded the appropriation from $2,000 to $3,000.

My estimate of $10,000, for the year 1857, is intended to

cover the above deficiencies, and to meet all necessary expenses under this head during the year.

This practice of exceeding appropriations has been carried to a culpable extent. It would seem that this habit of exceeding the appropriations of the legislature, for whatever purpose, should be rigidly discountenanced.

While the Bank and Insurance Commissioners doubtless render important service to the State, yet their expenses are increasing from year to year. The sum paid to the three Bank Commissioners for their services, clerk hire, and travelling expenses for twelve months to Oct. 1, 1856, was $6,983.85. During the same period the amount paid to the three Insurance Commissioners for their services, travelling expenses, clerk hire, rent of office, stationery and contingent office expenses, was $7,284.40. The estimates of $14,000 for these two departments, for the year 1857, are founded upon the expenses of last year.

The expenses of Commissioners for various purposes, have been much smaller than for the previous years. The sum paid in 1856, was $4,446.89. In my estimates for the year 1857, I have taken into consideration the fact that the Commissioners who have been engaged for the past two years in codifying the laws, may present claims for services rendered. The amount estimated for all Commissioners under this head, for the year 1857, is $10,000.

There has been paid from the treasury during the year 1856, on account of Indemnification to Officers, under the Act of 1855, chap. 271, $8,822.84. The time for commencing the suits under the above Act having expired, the amount for the present year will unquestionably be reduced, as the only claims which can now be presented for allowance, are for those cases already in court. I have, accordingly, estimated only $5,000 for 1857.

The amount paid to Sheriffs during the year 1856, for distributing blanks, school documents, proclamations, and returning votes, was $736.60. It cannot be expected that this service will be any less for the present year. I have therefore estimated for $800.

By the Resolve of 1820, chap. 18, the Secretary of State is directed to purchase 350 copies of the Reports of Decisions in the Supreme Court, for distribution among the cities and towns throughout the State. These, with other purchases under the Resolves of 1844, chap. 66, and 1848, chap. 23, for 1856, amounted to $2,214.10. The estimate for 1857, is $2,000.

There has been paid, on account of appropriations for the State Library, in accordance with Rev. Stat. chap. 11, sect. 12, and Resolves of 1854, chap. 76, 1856, chap. 27, during the past year, $3,692.76. The estimate for 1857, is $1,000.

The amount paid in 1856, for Weights, Measures and Balances furnished to new towns, under the Resolves of 1848, chap. 332, 1850, chap. 295, was $157. This sum being much smaller than usual, the estimate for 1857 is increased to $500.

There has been paid for the support of the Land Office during the past year, under the Act of 1851, chap. 190, $1,000. The same sum is estimated for 1857.

The Courts of Insolvency went into operation on the first of July last. The amount received into the State Treasury for the quarter ending September 30, 1856, as has been stated, was $195. The amount paid out for salaries and expenses, during the same period, was $7,124.43. As was to have been expected, the revenue is comparatively small. In my estimates for the receipts and expenditures for 1857, I have put down the probable receipts at $12,000. In justice to the courts, it is proper to state, that there was nothing to base the estimated receipts upon, save such information as I could obtain, and my own judgment. While the receipts may be more than doubled, yet they may not reach half that sum. The estimated expenditures are more accurate. The salaries for Judges and Registers are fixed by the Act of 1856, chap. 284, and amount to $27,800 a year. I have added for the expenses of the courts throughout all the counties, $6,200, making in all $34,000. If the above estimates prove correct, it will be seen that this system, compared with that which formerly prevailed, will add to the expenses of the State some $22,000 per annum. While the utility of these courts over the old system is apparent, yet it would seem that the salaries, in many cases, are disproportionate to the services rendered. Should the salaries be made to depend more upon the actual services rendered in the business transacted in the courts, no injustice would accrue to the parties interested, and at the same time the interest of the Commonwealth would be subserved in continuing the present system.

There was paid to the Attorney-General, under the Resolve of 1848, chap. 75, sect. 2, and charged to the account of " Legal Counsel," during the year 1856, the sum of $300, for the purpose of defraying his expenses while in attendance upon the suit pending in the Supreme Court of the United States, at Washington, between this Commonwealth and Rhode Island.

The amount paid to the Presidential Electors for 1856, authorized by the Rev. Stat. chap. 6, sect. 23, for services and travelling expenses, was $233.60.

There was paid in 1856, under the Act of 1856, chap. 48, $32,350.34, to the several cities and towns, as compensation to the agents employed by them in taking the Census and Statistics authorized by the Acts of 1855, chapters 439 and 467.

Charitable.

Under this head is included the appropriations for the Asylum for the Blind, School for Idiots, Asylum for the Deaf and Dumb, and the Eye and Ear Infirmary, amounting in all, for the year 1856, to $28,409.33. These institutions are noble tributes to our humanity and generosity, and while the citizens of our Commonwealth will always readily respond to every reasonable demand in their behalf, it behooves those having them in charge to exercise just prudence and economy in their management. The estimates for aid in the support of these institutions for 1857, are based upon those of last year, say $28,500.

There is likewise embraced under this head, the four State Almshouses, the three State Lunatic Asylums, State Paupers aided in various ways, and the support of Lunatics, amounting in the year 1856, to $246,289.17.

The expenses for the support of the inmates at the four State Almshouses in 1856, amounting to $173,565.13, exceeded, contrary to all expectations, the estimate of my predecessor. Every effort consistent with propriety and humanity, should be made to reduce the expenses of these establishments. Therefore, in view of the improved condition of the farms, and the expressed determination on the part of the Superintendents, to curtail the expenses if possible,—an effort as desirable as I believe it to be feasible,—the estimate for 1857 has been reduced to $170,000. If the Superintendents carry out successfully their designs, it is hoped that the estimate will prove much larger than the actual expenditure.

Believing that it might be of some interest, I have annexed the following table, showing the amount appropriated for the purchase of land and the buildings of the four establishments, exclusive of the land at Rainsford Island, and also the sums paid for the support of the inmates at each house, from the time they were opened for their reception, May 1, 1854, to Dec. 1, 1856, two years and seven months.

Appropriations for Lands and Buildings.

Bridgewater, ...	$86,710 76
Tewksbury, ...	89,843 28
Monson, ...	89,895 27
Rainsford Island, (exclusive of land,) . .	51,430 55
Building Commissioners, for services, . .	9,179 62
	$327,059 48
Less amount appropriated, unexpended Jan'y 1, 1857, ...	2,430 00
Whole outlay to Jan'y 1, 1857, . . .	$324,629 48

Expenses for the support of Inmates.

Bridgewater,	7 mos. to Dec. 1, 1854,	$14,806 10	
	12 " " " 1855,	29,962 18	
	12 " " " 1856,	33,091 72	
			$77,860 00
Tewksbury,	7 " " " 1854,	$28,043 15	
	12 " " " 1855,	56,685 99	
	12 " " " 1856,	51,919 14	
			136,648 28
Monson,	7 " " " 1854,	$23,692 69	
	12 " " " 1855,	49,312 11	
	12 " " " 1856,	53,515 97	
			126,520 77

Rainsf'd Isl'd, 7 mos. to Oct. 1 1854, $14,070 73
　　　　12 "　　　"　" 1855, 33,993 60
　　　　12 "　　　"　" 1856, 32,838 75
　　　　　　　　　　　　　　　　　　80,903 08

Inspectors, salaries and travelling ex-
　penses 1854,　.　.　.　.　$287 94
Inspectors, salaries and travelling ex-
　penses 1855,　.　.　.　.　2,604 89
Inspectors, salaries and travelling ex-
　penses in full to Oct. 1, 1856,　.　2,199 55
　　　　　　　　　　　　　　　　　　5,092 38

Whole expense for the support of inmates, .　.　$427,024 51
Add the cost of buildings to Jan'y 1, 1857,　.　324,629 48

Making, in all, .　.　.　.　.　.　.　$751,653 99

The amount paid in 1856, for salaries to the superintendents and officers of the Worcester and Taunton Lunatic Hospitals, was $5,845.98. The estimate for 1857, is $6,400. Learning that it is the intention of the trustees of the Northampton Lunatic Hospital to appoint a superintendent of that institution at an early day, I have estimated for salary on that account, for nine months of the present year, $1,000.

The sum paid in 1856 to the several cities and towns for the support, in sickness, burial and transportation, of paupers, and also that for the support of lunatics at the State and County Asylums, was $66,878.06. The cost for 1857 will probably be somewhat increased. I have estimated it at $75,000.

The bills of Coroners, amounting to $1,959.36 for the past year, are believed to be far more numerous and expensive than is necessary. Too many inquests are held, and many of these are prolonged to a needless and unjustifiable extent. Notwithstanding they are sworn officers of the Commonwealth, the charges of some of them are often exorbitant, and the settlement of their accounts is attended with a vast deal of difficulty. The evil is a growing one, and some action, if possible, should be taken for its remedy. My estimate for 1857, is $2,500.

The expenses for the support of Indians in the Commonwealth, has amounted during the year past, to $2,654.60. While our State, with characteristic justice and honesty, should ever extend its protecting arm over this hitherto much-abused portion of its population, yet as it is well known that many of their descendants are growing up in idleness, ignorance and vice, it is worthy of consideration whether, in justice to them, as well as to the Commonwealth, some method may not be applied to improve their condition in order that they may become industrious and useful citizens.   The estimate for 1857, is $3,000.

The expenses of the Alien Commissioners for 1856, amounting to $11,237.08, was larger than for the previous year.   This is owing to the passage of the Act of 1856, chap. 294, requiring one member of the Board to devote his whole time to the interests of the Commission.   A portion of the railroad agents have been discharged, and it is hoped that there will be no further occasion for their employment.   The estimated expenses for this department for the year 1857, is $10,000.

Under the Acts of 1852, chap. 275, sec. 13, and 1854, chap. 355, sec. 5, the sum of $6,000 is annually reserved from the amount received from Alien Passengers, to constitute a Sinking Fund for the redemption of scrip issued for the building of the three State Almshouses.

There was paid on account of Pensions the past year, $1,370.20.   The estimate for 1857, is $1,200

The amount paid during the year 1856, under the Resolve of 1841, chap. 65, on account of Annuities of Martha Johonnott, was $1,640.   The estimate for 1857, is $2,000.

Scientific and Educational.

Under this head is included Agricultural Societies, State Board of Agriculture, American Institute of Instruction, and State Maps and Surveys, the whole cost of which, for the year 1856, was $18,620.16.

It is proper to call attention to the fact, that there are now twenty-one Agricultural Societies drawing bounty from the State.   The amount paid from the treasury to these societies in 1856, was $11,634.76.   In some of the counties there are three, and in one, four societies.   Whether the interests of agriculture would not be as well subserved by limiting the number to one in each county, is a subject worthy of consideration.   If this reduction could be effected without injury to this most important branch of industry, it would tend to lessen somewhat the general expenditure. The estimate for 1857, is $12,000.

There has been expended by the Board of Agriculture, during the year 1856, under the Act of 1852, chap. 142, and the Resolves of 1856, chap. 65, 1853, chap. 67, 1854, chapters 72 and 88, the sum of $6,667.20, for improvements and experiments upon the State Farm, agricultural books, salary, clerk hire, and travelling expenses of the Secretary and of the Board. I am informed by the Secretary of the Board that a larger sum will be needed for this year. I have, therefore, put down as an estimate for 1857, $8,000.

There has been paid to the American Institute of Instruction the sum of $300, under the Resolve of 1855, chap. 36. This is an annual appropriation for five years, ending August, 1859.

The sum paid on account of State Maps and Surveys, under the Resolve of 1852, chap. 28, for the year 1856, was only $18.20. My estimate is $50 for 1857.

Military.

Under this head is included the Adjutant and Quartermaster-General's Department, Militia Bounty, Military Accounts, and the rent of Armories, the whole cost of which for the year 1856, was $75,147.84.

The above is exclusive of salaries, stationery, blanks, printing, and other office expenses, which, if added, would swell the amount to about $80,000 per annum.

The expenses of the Militia, although somewhat reduced from former years, would yet seem to be very large, considering the immediate benefits derived. Whether some means cannot be adopted by which this expenditure may be reduced, and at the same time not interfere, to any great extent, with the present excellent system, is a subject to which the attention of the legislature may properly be directed. One item of expenditure under this head, viz.: the rent of armories, which operates so unjustly and unequally under the present law, should, in my opinion, be so far modified as to place it upon the several cities and towns where the companies are located. This would relieve the State Treasury about $12,000 per annum, and might operate to rid the service of some companies in the towns where they are not needed, and which are of little use or credit to the Commonwealth. The estimated expense for 1857, is $76,000.

Reformatory and Correctional.

Under this head is included County Treasurers, Arrest of Fugitives, Reform School for Boys, Industrial School for Girls, Agent for Discharged Convicts, and Prevention of Counterfeiting, the whole expenses of which for the year 1856, amounted to $193,577.43.

The balances paid to County Treasurers, for two-thirds the costs of criminal prosecutions, are constantly increasing. The amount paid in 1856, was $135,134.45. These costs are made up by the District-Attorneys of the several districts, subject to the approval of their respective courts. There is no method at present by which the Auditor can ascertain the accuracy of these bills, and no alternative exists but to pay them as presented by the Treasurers, who I find upon inquiry, know quite as little of their correctness as does the Auditor. The truth is the District-Attorneys have the key to the State Treasury almost under their control, which may be used judiciously or not. It is the opinion of those most conversant with the facts, that it has not always been used with that care and prudence which its importance demands.

I have estimated the criminal costs for the year 1857, at $200,000, which sum is intended to cover about $42,000 claimed by the city of Boston, for expenses of criminal courts in the county of Suffolk, for nine months to July 1, 1856, and which has been withheld in consequence of the passage of the Act of 1855, chap. 449, establishing the Superior Court.

This account has not been paid from the fact that doubts existed in my own mind as to the legality of the claim, under the construction of the above Act. Similar doubts also existed, until very recently, on the part of those acting for the city.

Notwithstanding the large outlay for criminal costs throughout the State, and the necessity that exists of reducing all unreasonable expenditures, it would seem but just to the city of Boston that it should be placed upon an equal footing, in this

particular, with other parts of the Commonwealth. The atten
tion of the legislature is earnestly directed to this important
subject.

The expenses, amounting to $1,552.98, for the year 1856,
growing out of the arrest of fugitives from justice, have been
annually increasing. The agents employed under the warrants
do not, it is apprehended, always exercise that prudence and
economy in their execution which is desirable. There is a con-
stant pressure upon the Executive for these warrants, and it is
no doubt at times exceedingly difficult to judge as to the expediency or justice of issuing them. Misrepresentations are fre-
quently made to the Governor, in procuring warrants for the
arrest of persons who are not in reality fugitives, the object
being to gratify personal interests rather than to secure the
ends of public justice. It is manifest that, with the utmost
vigilance, which is always exercised on the part of the Executive, imposition to some extent, cannot be prevented. The
estimate for 1857, is $2,000.

The expenses for the support of the Reform School for Boys
are very large, amounting to $40,390 for the year 1856. When
it is considered that this institution has the advantages of one
of the best and most productive farms in the State, and its
resources in relation to labor are so great, which could be
employed a part of the time in the various mechanical as well
as agricultural branches, it would seem that the School should
do something more towards its own support. The estimate of
$42,960 for 1857, is based upon those of former years.

The Industrial School for Girls has recently gone into operation, and is, I believe, destined to become one of our most useful
institutions. While it adds another item to the expenditures,
it will be responded to most cheerfully if conducted with a due
regard to prudence and economy, as will doubtless be the case
under the management of the present able and careful Treasurer, and excellent Superintendent of the School. The expenses
for the year 1856, amounting in all to $13,000, have been for
the support of inmates, salaries, and for furniture for the three
buildings. The estimate for 1857, of $13,500, is based upon
the supposition that the present buildings, capable of accommo-
dating ninety inmates, will soon be filled, and that a larger

appropriation will be needed the present year in getting the institution fairly under way than will be wanted hereafter.

Under the Act of 1852, chap. 213, an annual appropriation, without limit, is made of $1,000, for salary and expenses of an agent in assisting Discharged Convicts.

The Resolve of 1852, chap. 76, appropriating $2,500, per annum for five years, in favor of the " Association of Banks for the Prevention of Counterfeiting," has expired, therefore no provision has been made for it in the estimates for 1857.*

Interest.

The item of Interest has been considerably augmented, on account of the increase of the Temporary Loan. The sum paid during the year 1856, was $152,222.19, an advance of $62,197.19 over that of the year 1855. The policy of this expenditure in a wealthy State like Massachusetts, and in a time of general business prosperity, may be considered of very doubtful expediency. The estimate for 1857, is $140,000.

Public Buildings.

Year after year large amounts of money have been expended, and, I might say, in some instances, squandered upon improvements and repairs of the various public buildings. The sum of $80,198.65 was expended for these purposes during the year 1856. As they are all at present in a good condition, it is doubtful whether a prudent economy would justify any considerable outlay upon them during the present year, and more particularly upon the four State Almshouses, the system of which is yet regarded as an experiment. These establishments have every convenience that can reasonably be desired, and all the buildings are in good order. It would seem that quite enough had already been expended upon them until it is decided that they shall become permanent institutions.

The Trustees of the Taunton Lunatic Hospital have made a

* Although the time for which the appropriation was made, under the Resolve, has expired, yet, as the Association has drawn but for four years, it is still entitled to one more payment unless the Act is repealed.

considerable outlay in providing the same with a heating and ventilating apparatus. The amount of $8,000, appropriated by the legislature of 1856, being insufficient for the purpose, the sum of $5,000 will be required to discharge the debt incurred in completing it. I am informed that the trustees proceeded with the work, and exceeded the amount appropriated, from the fact that the Committee on Charitable Institutions of last year justified the improvement, although they were aware that the sum appropriated was unequal to the completion of the proposed alterations, to the amount of the above sum.

The Commissioners for building the Northampton Lunatic Hospital, I am told, will ask for an appropriation of $50,000, for the purpose of a heating and ventilating apparatus, steam engine, barns, sheds, and other necessary fixtures in and about the building, preparatory to its occupancy. The trustees will also ask for an appropriation of $48,500, for the purpose of furnishing the building, stocking the farm, and erecting fences.

I would respectfully suggest, as a means of meeting the funded debt of the Commonwealth, now running to maturity, amounting in all, to $1,289,000, (including $150,000 scrip still unsold,) and which must be provided for by legislative action, that the legislature should authorize the Treasurer to borrow the School Fund, which amounts to $1,638,021.32, at such a valuation as they may think the character of the securities warrants, and at a rate of interest that will equal the present income of the fund, to redeem scrip whenever the payment of securities now in the School Fund enables him to do so.

The advantages claimed are, 1st. The extinction of the public debt, (which would seem the part of wisdom, as there is no necessity for its existence,) without recourse to the ordinary revenue. 2d. The income of the fund for educational purposes would be secure and permanent in its character, and definitely fixed, whereas it is at present subject to delay in the payment of interest on loans, and the fund itself to the losses incident to depreciated securities, which even now are considerable. 3d. The saving in labor, and consequently of expense in the management of the fund, and in the payment of interest on the Public Debt.

The policy of Sinking Funds is at least of doubtful wisdom,

and one to which no sagacious business man would think of
resorting as a means of paying debts. Such funds are liable to
losses from the failure of the securities in which they are placed,
which more than compensate for the advantages obtained.

I would suggest that no better investment can be found for
revenue devoted to the redemption of scrip, than in taking up
the scrip in anticipation of maturity.

All of which is respectfully submitted,

C. R. RANSOM, Auditor.

BALANCE SHEET, DECEMBER 31, 1856.

	DR.	CR.
Bank Tax, ...		$583,445 43
Insurance Tax, ...		3,305 98
State Tax, ...		584,884 45
Alien Passengers, ...		10,878 68
Attorney for Suffolk County, ...		529 97
Alien Estates, ...		966 77
Income Western Railroad Stock Sinking Fund,		52,852 10
Western Railroad Dividends, ...		49,392 00
Premium on 6 per cent. Scrip, 1856, . .		7,633 50
Interest on 6 per cent. Scrip, 1856, . . .	$3,750 85	
Interest on 5 per cent. Scrip, 1854. (Enlargement of State House,)	1,381 11	
Interest on 5 per cent. Scrip, 1854. (Lunatic Hospital and State Prison,) . . .	3,664 87	
Hawkers' and Peddler's Licenses, . . .		521 00
Per cent. on State Tax, ...		788 86
Annuity to Martha Johonnot, ...	1,640 00	
Blind Asylum, ...	12,000 00	
Council, ...	10,339 00	
Legislature, ...	199,155 53	
Salaries, ...	113,607 32	
Repairs, ...	16,615 69	
Furniture, ...	8,113 94	
Fuel and Lights, ...	2,647 97	
State Printing, ...	45,082 84	
Stationery, ...	7,748 73	
Postage, ...	1,583 87	
Newspapers, ...	8,854 61	
Index and Journals, ...	19,196 10	
Term Reports, ...	2,214 10	
Board of Agriculture, ...	6,667 20	
Agricultural Societies, ...	11,634 76	
American Institute of Instruction, . . .	300 00	
Indemnification of Officers, ...	8,322 84	
Legal Counsel, ...	300 00	

	DR.	CR.
Land Office,	$1,000 00	
Commissioners for various purposes,	4,446 89	
Bank Commissioners,	6,983 85	
Insurance Commissioners,	7,284 40	
Annuity to Harvard College,	666 66	
Asylum for Deaf and Dumb,	8,909 33	
School for Idiots,	5,000 00	
Eye and Ear Infirmary,	2,500 00	
Expenses of Taunton Lunatic Hospital,	3,070 98	
Expenses of Worcester Lunatic Hospital,	2,775 00	
Pensioners,	1,370 20	
Indians,	2,654 60	
Alien Commissioners,	11,237 08	
State Paupers,	66,843 14	
Expenses of State Almshouses,	173,565 13	
Sheriffs,	725 60	
Coroners,	1,959 36	
County Treasurers,	135,134 45	
Arrest of Fugitives,	1,384 23	
Agent for Discharged Convicts,	1,000 00	
Adjutant and Quartermaster-General's Dep't,	4,550 00	
Militia Bounty,	52,888 00	
Military Account,	5,782 13	
Rent of Armories,	11,877 31	
Expenses of Reform School,	40,390 00	
Contingent Fund,	2,500 00	
Prevention of Counterfeiting,	2,500 00	
Weights, Measures, and Balances,	157 00	
State Map and Survey,	18 20	
Interest,	48,726 50	
Interest on Scrip of 1850,	5,000 00	
" " Reform School,	5,000 00	
" ". 1852,	9,750 00	
" " Western Railroad,	49,725 00	
" " 1853 (State House),	3,250 00	
" " 1853 (Almshouse),	3,000 00	
" " 1853 (Lunatic Hospital),	3,675 00	
" " 1854 (Almshouse),	2,500 00	
Presidential Electors,	233 60	
Census and Statistics,	32,343 84	
Expenses of Industrial School,	13,000 00	
Courts of Insolvency,	6,929 43	
Worcester Hospital,	185,000 00	
Estate 12 Hancock Street,	12,500 00	
Arsenal at Cambridge,	281,754 18	
Charles River Bridge.	25,000 00	

	DR.	CR.
Warren Bridge,	$50,000 00	
Quit-claim due of M. Ambrose,	100 00	
School Fund for Indians,		$2,500 00
Yacht Whisper,	2,650 00	
Western Railroad Stock,	705,600 00	
"　　"　　" in School Fund,	376,500 00	
"　　"　　" in Stock S. Fund,	94,300 00	
Western Railroad Scrip sold,		995,000 00
"　　"　　" in School Fund,	190,000 00	
"　　"　　" in Stock S. Fund,	118,000 00	
Weights, Measures and Balances for General Government,	5,500 00	
Railroad Scrip loaned sundry Corporations,		5,049,555 56
Railroad Bonds and Mortgages,	5,049,555 56	
Rights of the Commonwealth in Western Railroad Loan Sinking Fund,	226,779 84	
Boston and Portland R. R. Scrip in School Fund,	50,000 00	
Eastern Railroad Scrip in School Fund,	20,000 00	
Rights of the School Fund in Western Railroad Loan Sinking Fund,	121,109 50	
Interest on School Fund for Indians,		75 00
Temporary Loan,		397,000 00
Norwich and Worcester Railroad Scrip in Stock Sinking Fund,	4,000 00	
Andover and Haverhill Railroad Scrip in Stock Sinking Fund,	2,000 00	
State House,	743,103 86	
Library,	17,046 09	
Reform School Fund,	20,000 00	
Massachusetts Claim,	181,000 00	
Reform School Scrip in Western R. R. Stock Sinking Fund,	89,202 28	
Reform School Loan,		100,000 00
Hassanamessett Indian Fund,		162 50
Rights of the Stock Sinking Fund in the Loan Sinking Fund,	80,808 02	
Loan of 1850,		100,000 00
Scrip of 1850 in Massachusetts School Fund,	4,000 00	
Natick Indian Fund,	1,125 15	
Reform School Scrip in School Fund,	10,797 72	
Lunatic Hospital and State Prison Scrip in School Fund,	17,000 00	
State House Scrip in School Fund,	10,000 00	
State Prison,	667,436 26	
Lunatic Hospital and State Prison Scrip in Stock Sinking Fund,	17,000 00	

	DR.	CR.
State House Scrip in Stock Sinking Fund,	$53,000 00	
Marshpee Indian Fund,	6,000 00	
Loan of 1852,		$100,000 00
Almshouse Loan of 1852,		100,000 00
State House Loan of 1853,		65,000 00
Almshouse Loan of 1853,		60,000 00
Lunatic Hospital Loan of 1853,		70,000 00
Western Railroad Stock Sinking Fund,		1,110,064 86
Notes and Mortgages,	282,935 23	
Notes and collateral,	265,000 00	
Maine 5 per cent. Scrip,	250,000 00	
Massachusetts School Fund,		1,638,021 33
Eastern Land Notes,	255,881 74	
Almshouse Scrip, 1853, in School Fund,	39,000 00	
Lunatic Hospital and State Prison Scrip in Almshouse Sinking Fund,	6,000 00	
State House Scrip in Almshouse Sinking Fund,	9,000 00	
Reform School,	163,000 00	
Almshouse Sinking Fund,		22,609 29
Charles River and Warren Bridge Fund,		2,301 68
Subscription to Reform School for Girls,		20,125 00
Todd Normal School Fund,		11,900 00
Interest on Todd Normal School Fund,		1 45
Almshouse Loan of 1854,		50,000 00
Lunatic Hospital and State Prison Loan, 1854,		94,000 00
Malden Bridge,	9,000 00	
Northampton Lunatic Hospital,	130,503 04	
State House Loan of 1854,		100,000 00
Commonwealth of Massachusetts,		1,480,669 03
State Almshouses,	324,629 48	
County, City and Town Scrip,	459,370 00	
Taunton Lunatic Hospital,	203,847 20	
Income of Massachusetts School Fund,		20,349 88
Industrial School,	41,927 13	
Loan of 1856,		300,000 00
Cash,	144,843 25	
Eastern Railroad,		3,100 00
Andover and Haverhill,		1,300 00
Norwich and Worcester,		10,500 00
	$13,199,433 77	$13,199,433 77

INDEX.